THE DAY THE KILLERS CAME

THE DAY THE KILLERS CAME

Wayne D. Overholser

Chivers Press • Thorndike Press
Bath, England   Waterville, Maine USA

This Large Print edition is published by Chivers Press, England, and by Thorndike Press, USA.

Published in 2002 in the U.K. by arrangement with the author, c/o Golden West Literary Agency.

Published in 2002 in the U.S. by arrangement with Golden West Literary Agency.

U.K. Hardcover ISBN 0–7540–4941–8 (Chivers Large Print)
U.K. Softcover   ISBN 0–7540–4942–6 (Camden Large Print)
U.S. Softcover   ISBN 0–7862–4190–X (Nightingale Series Edition)

The text of this Large Print edition is unabridged.
Other aspects of the book may vary from the original edition.

Set in 16 pt. New Times Roman.

Printed in Great Britain on acid-free paper.

British Library Cataloguing in Publication Data available

Library of Congress Cataloging-in-Publication Data

Overholser, Wayne D., 1906–
    The day the killers came / by Wayne D. Overholser.
       p.   cm.
    ISBN 0–7862–4190–X (lg. print : sc : alk. paper)
    1. Sheriffs—Fiction. 2. Large type books. I. Title.
    PS3529.V33 D39 2002
    813'.54—dc21   2002020717

CHAPTER ONE

Billy Horn was hungry and tired and thirsty, and what was worse, he was scared and mad. He was riding at the tag end of a line of ten men. He had been eating their dust for most of three days until it had worked through his pores and into his eyes and ears and nose. And for what? That question had been rawhiding him for most of the three days they'd been on the run since they'd held up the train near Casper.

More than a month ago Black Jack Conner had been released from Yuma prison. With the help of his old partner, Cutter Doon, he had put together a gang of ten men including Horn. 'We'll be rich in a month,' Black Jack had promised, 'and then we'll light out for Mexico and live like kings.'

It had sounded fine to young Horn who had just celebrated his twenty-third birthday by helping run a few steers out of Arizona into Mexico. He'd made peanuts on the deal, so when Black Jack showed up with Cutter Doon and the promise of big money, he'd jumped at the chance.

Horn had not known Black Jack personally, but he did know him by reputation. Before Black Jack had gone to Yuma, he'd been a skillful operator who had made big money. In

1

those days it had been considered a rare opportunity to ride with him, but something had happened while he was in Yuma. Horn and no one else in the outfit knew about it unless it was Cutter Doon, but the truth was Black Jack didn't care about big money. All he wanted to do was kill.

At first everything had gone fine. They'd hit two banks in Utah and got away with good hauls both times, then they'd made a long ride into central Wyoming and tackled the train just out of Casper. There was supposed to be $100,000 in the express car, but somebody had given Black Jack the wrong information. They had found nothing in the express car—absolutely nothing.

The part that got to Horn was the brutal fact that Black Jack had killed two men in the first Utah holdup and three in the second. For no reason, either. Horn had no qualms about killing a man if it was a question of getting away or being caught, but to kill for the fun of killing was something else.

It made Horn a little sick. Besides, it was stupid. All you did was to make the law more anxious to catch up with you, and the posse that had been on their trail for the last three days was anxious enough anyway. But then, maybe that was because Black Jack had killed five men when they'd held up the train.

Here they were, riding through the Wyoming hills on lathered horses that had just

2

about reached the end of the line. If they didn't find fresh mounts at the next ranch, or in the little town of Platte City which wasn't far ahead, they'd all be on foot.

Every time Horn thought about it, he put a hand to his neck. He could feel the rope tighten now. That was why he was scared. He was mad because of the killings. There would be more, too. Horn could count on that. They were going to knock over the Platte City bank at noon and Black Jack wouldn't miss a chance.

They topped a ridge. Ahead of them was a small valley. A ranch was in the bottom, the first one they'd seen for miles. The hour was still early, the sun barely showing over the next ridge to the east. Horn sighed. He had never been so tired in his life. Three days of riding, of circling and backtracking and stopping only long enough to give the horses a little rest.

Platte City was about another mile to the east, so they'd have to stop here for a few hours, Horn told himself. Otherwise they'd get to Platte City long before noon. At least he'd get a drink and maybe a square meal. It had been a long time since his belly had been full.

The ranch wasn't much, Horn saw as they rode past the corral toward the shack, just a ten-cow spread set out here in the sagebrush. More of a farm than a ranch, with a big garden and an irrigation ditch that ran on the other side of the hen house, and a pigpen yonder

3

that stunk so much Horn wondered how anybody could stand it.

Black Jack reined up and signalled for the others to stop. For a moment he sat his saddle and just looked around, then as he dismounted, he said, 'Don't look like much. Chances are we won't find any horses here worth taking.'

The men stepped down. Black Jack motioned for Cutter Doon to go with him to the shack. Horn remained beside his sweat-gummed horse and watched the two men walk to the front door. Black Jack was average height, but he looked shorter because he was so broad-shouldered. He had a huge head, and his neck was the size of a corner fence post. He was as big as a Hereford bull. He wasn't like a bull, though. He was more like a weasel, Horn thought. Or a wolverine. Mean. Just plain mean all the way down from his big head to his boot heels.

Black Jack and Cutter were within ten feet of the open door when an old man stepped out, a cocked, double-barreled shotgun in his hands. He was frail and skinny and stooped with rheumatism, but there was still plenty of fire in his faded blue eyes. He barked, 'That's far enough. What do you want?'

Black Jack would probably have shot him then and there if he hadn't held the shotgun, Horn thought. He glared at the old man for a moment, then he said, 'We want breakfast. We

4

likewise need horses. We're going to stay here until noon, but we want to eat as soon as we take care of our horses.'

'You go to hell,' the old man said, pointing the shotgun directly at Black Jack's barrel of a chest. 'I don't have enough grub in the house to feed a bunch as big as yours. I wouldn't cook breakfast for you if I did, and I've only got two horses. I sure ain't giving 'em to you.'

'I'm Black Jack Connor. You want to say it over, real slow?'

'No,' the old man snapped. 'I don't want to say it over. I don't care if you're Black Jack or Red Jack or Jack Ass. Just get on your horses and slope out of here. You can get breakfast in Platte City, and maybe you can trade Carl Sturtz out of some horses.'

'Well now,' Black Jack, his tone deceptively mild, 'I was hoping you could be reasonable, but since you ain't, we've got to play it our way.'

Cutter Doon had moved away from Black Jack. Now, without warning, his right hand came up very fast with his gun. He fired just as Black Jack moved in the opposite direction away from the muzzle of the shotgun.

The old man was slammed back against the front wall of the cabin, his finger pulling the trigger involuntarily, the buckshot flying harmlessly into space. For a moment his body was held upright by the wall, the shotgun slipping out of his hands, then his knees

5

buckled and he went down.

Black Jack motioned to Horn. 'Drag his carcass around to the back. I don't want to stumble over it all morning. Cutter will cook up a bait of breakfast. The rest of you rub the horses down. Feed 'em whatever you can find. Take a look at the old man's horses in the corral to see if they're worth taking.'

'We ain't goin' very far on these horses,' Cutter Doon said. 'They'll drop dead in another five miles.'

'We'll pick up some fresh animals in Platte City,' Black Jack said. 'If they ain't got a livery stable in town, we'll have to ride these horses. They'll get three, four hours rest, before we start for town.'

'Who's this Carl Sturtz he was talking about?' Cutter Doon asked. 'He said, maybe we could swap with him.'

'How the hell would I know?' Black Jack answered irritably. 'Maybe he's got the livery stable.'

Horn had dragged the body around the corner of the shack and had returned. Now he asked, 'How long will it take us at the bank?'

' 'Bout five minutes,' Black Jack answered. 'We'll hit it right at noon. We won't have no trouble. Everybody'll be at the state fair at Douglas. There won't be ten people in town.' He pulled at his mustache, his dark eyes narrowing as he asked, 'You scared, Horn?'

He gave it as a challenge, direct and wicked,

6

and for, a moment Horn was tempted to accept it. He was quitting the outfit before long, and he wasn't sure he could do it before he had it out with Black Jack.

He hated the man enough to kill him and he was convinced he could take him. In the old days Black Jack had been very fast, but the years had slowed him. The trouble now was that Cutter would jump into the fight and Horn knew he couldn't take both men.

Horn shrugged, deciding there would be a better time. He said, 'Oh, I'm scared, all right, but not of what you think I am. I'm scared we won't find anything in the tin can safe the bank's got. It may work like the train we tackled.'

Horn had returned the challenge. Now Black Jack could pick it up or reject it. He hesitated, scowling, his gaze sweeping the semicircle of men standing behind Horn. He must know, Horn thought, that the train robbery rankled in the mind of every man here. Another failure and he'd lose his outfit. They'd all know, as Horn did, that Black Jack had lost his touch.

'We'll get something,' Black Jack said. 'Put the horses up.' He jerked his head at Cutter Doon. 'Come on. Let's rustle some grub.'

Horn grinned as he led his horse to the water trough beside the corral gate. Two other men had taken Black Jack's and Cutter's horses as well as their own. Horn sloshed water over his face, and as he straightened up, the man beside him said, 'Billy, you're going out of your way to kick up trouble with Jack. You'll find some if you don't watch out.'

Horn wiped water from his face and blew out a great breath. 'Peewee, if we miss out in Platte City, I'm going to find some. Maybe you don't know it, but we're about finished.'

The other man nodded. 'I know it, all right. Looks to me like Black Jack's a has been.'

'He's a killer,' Horn said bitterly. 'That's all he is, and it takes more'n that to ride the owlhoot these days.'

He took his time with his horse, then rolled and smoked a cigarette. He knew he would be a better leader than Black Jack Connor, and for the first time he thought seriously about taking the gang away from Black Jack. By the time he started toward the house, he decided he'd wait to call for a showdown. Maybe Platte City would be the right place if they found the safe empty.

When Horn reached the shack, he heard Black Jack say, 'It sure looks to me if the old man had somebody else living with him, but it wasn't no woman. Ain't enough foofaraw for that, so it must have been another man. Now maybe he went to Douglass to see the fair, but maybe he's hiding in one of the other buildings. Go out and take a good look in the woodshed and the privy and the hen house. The pigpen, too.'

Horn found what they were hunting in the hen house. When he returned to the shack, he said, 'It's my guess somebody was cleaning out the hen house when we rode up. The hoe's on the floor where he left it, and the drop boards about half cleaned off.'

'So he must have seen us and ran,' Cutter said. 'Funny we didn't see him.'

Black Jack frowned as he thought about it, then he said, 'It don't change nothing. We've got to eat and the horses have got to rest. Besides, there won't be enough men in Platte City to worry us none.'

Horn pinned his gaze on Black Jack's dark face. He was the youngest man in the outfit, and he was convinced he was the smartest. It wasn't brains that would impress these men as much as guts, and Horn knew that if he was going to take Black Jack's place, he had to demonstrate just how much guts he had.

'Jack, it looks to me like you'd have been smart to have had the place searched when we got here,' Horn said.

The implication was plain enough, and Black Jack was tempted to pick up the challenge this time. He hesitated, his right hand splayed above the butt of his gun, then he said, 'Horn, you ain't dry behind the ears yet, and everybody knows it but you. Now shut your damned mouth.'

Black Jack turned to the stove where Cutter Doon was frying eggs. Horn grinned and winked at Peewee. Black Jack had got out of a showdown that time by pointing to Horn's youth. The only thing to do was to wait. All that Black Jack needed to hang himself was a little more time and plenty of rope.

CHAPTER TWO

Young Chuck Morgan, staring through the cobweb-covered window in the hen house, watched Black Jack Connor's gang ride up and dismount and shoot his grandfather down in cold blood. His first reaction was one of blind rage and a crazy desire to run out of the hen house and kill every one of them.

If he'd had a gun, he would have tried it, but he stopped after taking two steps. He held the hoe over his shoulder by the handle as if it were a baseball bat. Not much of a weapon. This was stupid. They'd shoot him down just as they had his grandfather.

So Chuck waited, his heart thumping and sweat pouring down his face. He was nagged by the thought that this wasn't real. It must be a nightmare. He was probably still sleeping in his bunk at one end of the shack and Grandpa was trying to wake him up, but he didn't want to wake up. He squeezed his eyes shut, hoping it would go away, but when he opened them, nothing had changed. The tired, lathered horses and ten hard cases standing in front of the shack and his grandfather's body lying there beside the door. No, this was real enough.

Presently one of the outlaws dragged Chuck's grandfather's body around the corner of the shack. A little later two of them went inside and the other eight led their horses to the corral. As they passed the hen house, Chuck made out some of the talk, enough to know what was going to happen. *They were headed for Platte City to rob the bank at noon.*

Chuck felt as if he had been hit on the head with a club. He was too stunned to think clearly, but one thing dug into his consciousness. He had to get to town and warn the people about what was going to happen.

There wouldn't be more than six or eight people in Platte City at noon today. Almost everybody had gone to Douglas to the state fair but Chuck's girl, Betsy Mills, would still be there, and so would his friend, Johnny Roan, who worked for old skinflint Jake Warner, the Platte City banker. Betsy might not get hurt, but they'd kill Johnny just as they'd killed Chuck's grandfather.

But how was he going to get out of the hen house so he could go to town? They'd smoke him down the second he stepped into the yard. They might decide to search the hen house. They'd find him if he stayed and they'd kill him.

11

Chuck wiped a hand across his face. It came away wet. He couldn't do anything for Grandpa, but he could do something for himself and Johnny Roan who would be alone in the bank. Jake Warner always went to Douglas to the state fair.

Then he thought about Betsy with her bright blue eyes and honey-colored hair and cheeks as red as a ripe Winesap, and he thought about what men like these would do to a pretty girl like Betsy. Tears came into his eyes as he clenched his fists. He *had* to get out of here and go to town.

The problem was escaping from the hen house. The door opened on the side away from the shack, but the men at the corral would see him. If he could reach the irrigation ditch which ran on past the hen house and the shack to the top of the ridge, he could crawl along it without being seen. The weeds on both sides of the ditch were high enough to hide him if he stayed low.

He shook his head. It wasn't more than ten feet from the hen house door to the ditch, but that ten feet might as well have been a mile. The men at the corral could see him if they were looking in his direction, and he'd be a fool to expect all eight of them to have their backs to him while he made the dash from the door to the ditch.

For a moment he was tempted to stay here in hopes they'd eat and ride on, but the next moment he thought about Betsy and about Johnny Roan who had a wife and baby. He couldn't stay. He rubbed his sweaty palms along his pants leg and told himself he might just as well try for the ditch.

Then the men began stringing back to the shack from the corral and he heaved a long, sighing breath, weak with relief. Funny he hadn't thought of that before. In a little while they'd all go to the shack for breakfast.

But the next few minutes were the longest in his life. He counted five men walk past the hen house, then six, then seven, but the last one took a long time with his horse. After he finished, he stood beside the corral gate and rolled and smoked a cigarette as if he were thinking about something.

Finally he turned and walked back to the shack, throwing his cigarette stub into the grass. The instant he disappeared through the door, Chuck slipped out of the hen house and lunged toward the ditch.

For a time Chuck lay flat on his belly in the mud in the bottom of the ditch, breathing hard and listening, but he heard nothing from the shack. He crawled frantically toward the ridge and still it seemed he was moving too slowly. He couldn't risk going any faster. If he did, he'd be on his hands and knees with his rump or shoulders showing above the weeds and they'd probably spot him

He lost track of time. He wasn't even sure

13

where he was or whether he could risk crawling out of the ditch. Presently he discovered that the ditch was level, so he must have reached the top of the ridge. He rolled over the east bank and kept rolling. When he thought he had dropped far enough over the crest so he wouldn't be seen, he got to his hands and knees and crawled. A few minutes later he jumped up and ran.

The town was just ahead of him now, a scattering of buildings strung out along Main Street, with most of the dwellings facing side streets that paralleled Main. The old stone jail that had been built years ago and hadn't been used for a long time was on the south side of Main Street.

The fire bell hanging in a twenty-foot tower stood beside the jail. Chuck knew he'd have everybody in town running toward the bell the minute he rang it. They'd think the town was on fire and it might be, too, after these men cleaned out the bank.

Chuck started to run faster and stumbled and fell headlong. For a little while he couldn't move. He lay there panting, sucking air into his tortured lungs, and all the time he had the goading thought that he had to get back on his feet and keep running. Maybe they wouldn't wait until noon; maybe they'd head for town as soon as they finished eating breakfast.

He got up and went on, trotting instead of running because the strength wasn't in him now. He didn't see anyone on the street, but that was to be expected. It was still early in the morning, and with almost everyone in Douglas for the fair, there was little need for the people who were still here to be on the street.

When he reached the jail, he untied the rope that was attached to the bell and pulled. The clang of the old bell was far from musical, but it was loud and could be heard by everyone all over town, particularly now during the warm weather when doors and windows were open.

Chuck was still panting, but his breath was coming easier and he kept on pulling. Betsy Mills and her mother ran out of the Bon Ton Café into the street. Mrs. Mills owned the café and she and her daughter lived in the back of the building. Betsy worked for her mother during the summer and on week ends and after school during the winter. Now they looked up and down the street. Not seeing any smoke, they ran toward the bell.

Baldy Mack stepped out of his store which was next to the jail, then Limpy Smith left his saloon across the street, bawling, 'Where the hell is the fire? I don't see no fire.'

Chuck didn't answer, but kept on ringing the bell. He saw Johnny Roan turn into Main Street and race toward him. Johnny was wearing his black suit and white shirt and tie even though the day would be a hot one. He always wore his suit in the bank because Jake

15

Warner said a cashier had to appear dignified.

A short time later they reached the bell, Johnny asking, 'Where's the fire, Chuck?'

'Yeah, what kind of a practical joke is this, young man?' Mrs. Mills demanded. 'There isn't any fire, is there? What are you up to?'

Betsy, standing beside her mother, stared at Chuck's shirt and pants. 'Chuck, how in the world did you get all that mud on you?' she asked.

'I'd like to know about that, too,' Mrs. Mills said. 'It looks to me like you could take the trouble to clean up before you come to town.'

Chuck ignored her. He didn't make any effort to answer Betsy's question, either. The deputy, old Carl Sturtz, had not showed up yet. He wasn't much of a law man, but he was the only one Platte City had, so Chuck wanted him to know what was happening. As for Mrs. Mills, all she had to do to make him mad was to open her mouth. She didn't like him. He guessed it was because he wanted to marry Betsy, and Mrs. Mills didn't want to lose her cheap help in the café.

Johnny Roan, impatient because Chuck wasn't answering their questions, shook Chuck's shoulder. 'What's the matter with you?' he demanded. 'If there isn't any fire, something must have happened.'

'It did,' Chuck said. 'Where's the deputy? Did he go to the fair?'

'No, I don't think so,' Johnny said. 'I'll go

16

get him.'

Chuck nodded and kept on ringing the bell as Johnny crossed the street to the livery stable.

CHAPTER THREE

Carl Sturtz had lived about as exciting a life as a man could. He had been marshal in several Kansas trail towns, he'd scouted for the army during the last campaign against the Sioux, and he'd been a United States Marshal. He had known personally several of the most famous men of the West including Hickock, Masterson and the Earps. He had been in Deadwood when Hickock was killed.

Now age had caught up with him and he was the first to admit it. His wife said caustically that he was about forty years late settling down. He bought the livery stable in Platte City and built a four-room house a block away, and did indeed settle down to a dull life. His wife's constant bitching didn't alter the dullness.

About a year ago Abe Newel, the sheriff in Douglas, rode to Platte City and told Sturtz he needed a deputy who lived here and he wanted Sturtz to take the star. Sturtz replied that he was old and tired and couldn't draw a gun very fast any more and he couldn't ride a horse all day if he had to bring in a wanted man.

The sheriff said that made no never mind to him. Sturtz had the savvy and that was all it took to handle the usual things that came up in a small town like Platte City. Platte City had the stone jail. It hadn't been used for a while, but it would still hold anyone Sturtz had to arrest.

Actually, Newel confided, the chances were Sturtz wouldn't have anything to do. It was just that Jake Warner and Baldy Mack and some of the other business men thought there should be a law man in Platte City.

Sturtz pulled on his pipe and thought about it. He remembered that in the three years he had lived in Platte City there had never been any crime committed worse than having a bunch of cowboys ride into town and let off steam by shooting at the sky. He told Newel he'd take the star.

Since then his life had not become exciting, but it was more interesting. He could walk down the street with the star pinned on his vest, all bright and shiny in the sunlight. People like young Johnny Roan and Betsy Mills would stop and pass the time of day and call him 'Deputy.' It was a small thing, but it was a mark of respect, a little bit like calling an old Civil War veteran 'Colonel' when he hadn't made anything higher than corporal.

This had been a good week because Sturtz's wife was in Douglas for the fair. She was a

18

great one for keeping her fingers busy every minute and she thought Sturtz should keep his busy, too. She took an angel food cake, some embroidery, and a red-and-white afghan to the fair.

As far as Sturtz was concerned, it was a great thing for his wife to be in Douglas. She lived by the clock and he was never allowed to sleep during the day. Now, just as an act of defiance, Sturtz rose early, took care of the horses in the livery stable, and returned to the house and cooked breakfast. Then he went back to bed. He was sound asleep when Chuck Morgan began ringing the fire bell.

It took a while for Sturtz to wake up, and after he woke up, it took a little longer for him to recognize the noise that had wakened him. When he did, he jumped out of bed and pulled on his pants and boots, thoroughly scared because the weather had been very dry. He had seen more than one western town destroyed by fire. With almost everyone gone, there wasn't much chance a fire could be stopped.

If he lost the livery stable . . . He ran out of the house and across the street to the livery stable. He raced the length of the runway to Main Street, and that was when he saw Chuck Morgan pulling on the bell. He slowed to a walk and sighed in relief. He had no idea why Chuck was ringing the bell, but it seemed unlikely that he was signaling a fire.

19

Sturtz crossed Main Street as Johnny Roan turned back to Chuck Morgan. Chuck must have been ringing the bell longer than Sturtz thought because Baldy Mack was here, too, along with Betsy Mills and her mother. That was everybody in town except Mrs. Johnny Roan and her baby and Mrs. Mack.

'He wouldn't tell us what happened until you got here,' Johnny Roan said.

Sturtz nodded. He stopped in front of Chuck who had stopped ringing the bell. He saw that the boy was under an emotional strain of some sort, so he waited until Chuck was ready to talk.

Chuck swallowed, wiped a dirty sleeve across his eyes, and took a long breath, then he blurted. 'A bunch of outlaws rode up this morning and murdered Grandpa. They're coming into town at noon to rob the bank.'

They stared at Chuck, unable to fully grasp what he had said. It was incredible, so incredible that it was hard to believe. Sturtz was the first to recover. He asked, 'How many were there, Chuck?'

'Ten.'

'You know what outfit it is?'

'The man who talked to Grandpa said he was Black Jack Connor. They called the one who done the shooting Cutter.'

Sturtz's breath went out of him. He had known Black Jack a long time ago when the outlaw was just a punk kid. During his years of

20

dealing with law breakers, he had never known anyone who was so completely devoid of all decent human characteristics.

But he didn't tell them that. He said, 'Black Jack's a bad one. He's been in the Arizona pen and I hadn't heard he was out. You know, I'll bet this is the bunch that held up the train over by Casper.'

No one said anything for a good part of a minute, then Sturtz realized they were looking at him as if expecting him to go out to the Morgan farm and capture the gang single-handed. Then, for the first time since he had taken the star, he told himself he should have given it back to Abe Newel. He was too old to buck a hard case like Black Jack.

'How'd you get away?' Sturtz asked.

'I was in the hen house when they rode up,' Chuck answered. 'They didn't know I was there. I watched 'em and heard what they said to Grandpa. I seen 'em shoot him. They had almost ridden their horses to death and they were hungry and talking about sleeping this morning. While they were eating breakfast, I sneaked over to the ditch and crawled along it till I got past the cabin, then I ran to town.'

'I know Black Jack,' Sturtz said, 'and I've heard about Cutter. They ain't like Butch Cassidy and his Wild Bunch. They're crazy. At least Black Jack and Cutter are. Crazy enough to rape any woman they can find and kill any man they see just for the fun they get out of

21

killing. I'd say there was a good chance they'll burn the town.'

'Horsefeathers,' Mrs. Mills snorted. 'You're an old man full of lies and you're scared. I don't believe you know anything about 'em.'

Sturtz understood why Betsy's father had died. It had been the best and most final way of escape from being Mrs. Mills' husband. He turned to Johnny Roan, ignoring Elsie Mills. 'I'll saddle up and ride to Douglas as fast as I can. I might get back by noon with the sheriff and a posse. Meanwhile you folks have got to decide what you're going to do.'

'We'll leave town,' Chuck said. 'No sense staying here and getting killed.'

'Where would we go?' Johnny demanded.

'Anywhere,' Chuck answered.

Johnny shook his head. 'I can't take my wife and baby anywhere. I can't go off and leave the money for them to take, either, but I can take it out of the safe and hide it so they can't find it.'

Baldy Mack nodded agreement. 'I'm voting with you, Johnny.' He motioned to the jail. 'I'd feel safer holed up right in there than I would riding away from here. I don't figure they'll stay in town after they find out the money's gone. Chances are they'll take the horses out of the livery stable and girt.'

'If they get any idea about burning the town,' Johnny said, 'we'll fire a few shots at 'em and hurry 'em along.'

22

Mrs. Mack had come up and was standing behind her husband. Now she stepped forward and said, 'I say the same. Baldy'n me have worked hard all our lives. We don't have nothing but the store. Maybe we can't save it, but I ain't gonna run away and let 'em have it for the taking.'

'We can move enough food and water into the jail so we won't suffer,' Johnny said. 'It's going to be hot, but we can stand it for one day. I'll go home and get Clara and the baby.'

'I'll fetch some grub from the house,' Mrs. Mack said. 'Baldy, you get all the guns and ammunition we've got in the store and move it into the jail. That's the first thing they'll look for. They may take some supplies, but we can stand that.'

They would do more than that, Sturtz thought. Black Jack was the kind who would ruin and burn just for the sake of the burning and ruining regardless of who owned it or the good it would do him and his gang of outlaws. But no one would understand that or even believe it until they saw it. Like Mrs. Mills, he thought resentfully, they would say he was a scared old man full of lies.

'I'll get started,' Sturtz said. 'One thing. Don't shoot the minute you see them. If you plug one of 'em, they'll know right off where you are and they'll stay and fight.'

Limpy Smith was staring at him speculatively as if not sure whether to believe it or not. Mrs. Mills had changed her mind about him. That was plain enough from the expression on her big, ugly face. He wheeled and ran back across the street, telling himself he'd never eat another meal in the Bon Ton as long as he lived.

Then he laughed, remembering he had only eaten one meal there since he had moved to Platte City. Suddenly he felt good, better than he had for years. He'd get back from Douglas in time to help fight Black Jack's bunch. He hadn't heard the whine of bullets or smelled powdersmoke for a long time. The thought was enough to make a young man out of him.

He saddled his buckskin and ran into the house. He buckled his gun belt around him, grabbed his Winchester off the antler rack near the front door, and ran back to his horse. He rammed the rifle into the boot and, stepping into the saddle, gave the buckskin a cut with the end of the reins. He left town on the dead run, knowing it would be close if he got back here with a posse by noon.

CHAPTER FOUR

For a moment after Carl Sturtz disappeared into the livery stable, no one in the group by the fire bell moved or said a word. It was a strange kind of tension, Johnny Roan thought.

There was much to be done and none of them knew whether there was time enough to do it. Still, they were held there in a sort of paralysis, afraid of what was going to happen and yet knowing they had to face it.

Johnny looked at Limpy Smith, suddenly feeling uneasy. He was unable to decide what was in the saloon man's mind. Smith stood staring at the archway of the livery stable, frowning thoughtfully as if he wasn't quite sure what he was going to do. Then without a word of explanation to anyone, he started back across the street toward his saloon.

Smith's action broke the tension. Johnny called, 'Limpy, what are you going to do?'

Smith turned, grinning. 'Well sir, I'm going back to my place of business and I'm going to stay there. If you gents want to hole up in that damned oven and stay there all day, it's your business, but it's my business what I do.'

'You idiot,' Chuck Morgan said angrily. 'Didn't you hear what we just said? Or do you think I made it up?'

'Oh, I believe you, all right,' Smith said, 'but that don't mean I'm scared of 'em. I figure they'll come to my saloon as soon as they hit town. They'll be thirsty, so I might just as well be on hand to sell 'em what they want. If I ain't on hand to sell 'em the liquor, they'll take it anyway.

Johnny stared at the man, unable to believe what he had heard. He said, 'Limpy, have you gone out of your head? These men are killers. You heard what Chuck said they did to his grandpa. You heard what Sturtz said about 'em, that they'd kill a man just for the sake of killing.'

'They won't kill me.' Smith waved Johnny's warning away with a sweep of his hand. 'Sure I heard, but nobody kills a saloon man. I'm a sort of servant to mankind you might say, pouring their whisky and listening to their troubles. These outlaws will have plenty of trouble to tell me. You can bet your bottom dollar on that.'

He turned again. Johnny swore under his breath. He wasn't going to argue with Smith about it. If the saloon man wanted to get his head shot off, it was his business just as he had said, but Baldy Mack couldn't let it go.

'Limpy, you know we've got to stick together if we're not all going to get killed,' Mack said hotly. 'There ain't many of us left in town, and there's no telling when Sturtz will get back with help, or if he will ever get back with any help.'

'That's right,' Chuck said, his gaze on Betsy. 'We've got women and a baby to think of, but seems like you ain't thinking of nothing except the few stinking dollars you're gonna make selling whisky to a bunch of murderers.'

'Well sonny,' Smith said, 'a dollar from a bunch of murderers goes just as far as one from a good man like you, and I ain't noticed

26

any of you spending many dollars in my place. I'll tell you this. Nobody ever looked out for Limpy Smith but Limpy Smith. My business ain't been real good lately. This looks like my chance to make some dinero.'

'But we need you . . .' Chuck began.

'To hell with anybody else needing me,' Smith snarled. 'You don't have to stay in town. Get out while you've got time.'

He turned away. Nobody said a word to stop him as he walked on across the street to his saloon. Then Baldy Mack blew out a long breath and said, 'I'll never buy another drink from that bastard.'

'It'll serve him right if that bunch shoots him full of holes,' Chuck said angrily. 'I never had much use for him, but I didn't think . . .'

'Well,' Mrs. Mills said in her usual belittling tone, 'I know exactly how he figures. I ain't had much business lately, neither. I sure ain't had none from any of you, or that worn-out old Carl Sturtz, neither. Now that I've got a chance to sell some hot dinners, I'm going to take it. I don't blame Limpy one bit. It's like he said. If I ain't on hand to cook for 'em and get paid, they'll rustle their dinner themselves. What's more, if you scaredy cats are afraid of these men, you don't have to stay here. Come on, Betsy.'

'She ain't going with you,' Chuck said as he grabbed Betsy's arm. 'She's going to stay with us.'

'Well, listen to that young rooster crow,' Mrs. Mills said, and laughed. 'You ain't dry behind the ears, but you're telling me what my daughter's going to do?'

She took a step toward Betsy and reached out to grip her other arm. Johnny's pulse started to pound. First Limpy Smith and now Elsie Mills. He stepped forward so he stood between her and Betsy, and with a sharp downstroke of his right hand, slapped Mrs. Mills' extended arm to one side.

'Go ahead and let them rape you if they can stand doing it,' Johnny said, 'but you're not taking Betsy and putting her up for bait.'

She whirled on Johnny, drawing her right arm back to slap him in the face, then hesitated as if seeing something in him she had never seen before.

Johnny said, 'I never hit a woman in my life, but you lay a hand on me and I'll knock you pizzle end up. I never liked you much anyhow, knowing the way you treat Betsy and the way you treated my wife when she worked for you, but right now I like you a hell of a lot less than I ever did. I figure you deserve whatever they do to you.'

'They're right,' Mrs. Mack said. 'You can't take Betsy into your café and risk what a wolf pack like that might do to her. Come on, Betsy. Help me round up some grub and we'll move it into the jail.'

'Of all the damned gall,' Elsie Mills said,

thoroughly outraged. 'Betsy's my girl. She ain't yours.' She glared at Mrs. Mack, then swung around to face Chuck. 'You've been following her around looking like a wall-eyed calf. You'd better start looking the other way because she ain't for the likes of you. I ain't no snivelling coward, neither. These men will rob the bank and buy a drink or two from Limpy and a hot dinner from me and then ride on. They're too smart to go around burning towns and raping women. Now come on, Betsy, and help me. We've got some pies to bake.'

Betsy shook her head. 'I'm not going, Ma. They're right. You can do what you want to, but you can't make me . . .'

'Oh, so I can't make you,' Mrs. Mills said, her face turning red. 'Why, you young idiot, I'm doing you a good turn and you don't have sense enough to know it. That jail will be an oven before noon. You stay in it all day and you'll wish you were in my cool kitchen helping me bake pies.'

Betsy shook her head again, her lips squeezed tightly together. She faced Mrs. Mack. 'Let's go get that grub. Those men might not wait until noon, and we're standing around jawing and doing nothing.'

Mrs. Mack nodded and, turning, walked toward her house. Betsy hesitated, her eyes on her mother, then she followed Mrs. Mack. For a moment Elsie Mills seemed unable to grasp the fact that for the first time in her life Betsy was actually defying her, then she whirled to face Johnny.

'I never seen a man or a bunch of men I couldn't handle,' she said hotly. 'I ain't afraid of this Black Jack and the rest of them. If you so-called men had any guts at all, you'd go ahead with your business. Except for the bank, you won't be bothered. When Betsy comes crawling back to me, I'll larrup her good. And I'll get even with you, Roan. You, too, Morgan. Don't you ever come sucking around after Betsy again or I'll give you a load of buckshot.'

She trudged back toward her café, kicking up a cloud of dust with every step. If the situation had been different, Johnny Roan would have laughed.

'I'll go home and get Clara and the baby,' Johnny said. 'Then I'll come back and move the money. It's like Betsy said. We've spent too much time standing here augering.'

Baldy Mack nodded. 'You never know about people,' he said. 'Not until you get in a squeeze and they have to stand up and be counted. Come on, Chuck. We've got a lot of work to do.'

Johnny strode home, thinking Baldy Mack was right about people. You just didn't know. Then he wondered bleakly about Jake Warner. Would the tightwad thank him for saving the bank's money? Probably not, he thought bitterly. The old man would likely expect him to stand behind the counter and keep open for business just on the chance the outlaws would deposit their money in the bank before they rode on.

CHAPTER FIVE

Johnny went into the house through the front door and, hearing Clara singing in the kitchen, crossed the living room into the kitchen. Clara heard him. Startled, she turned from the stove where she was stirring a tapioca pudding. Billy, sitting in his high chair by the window, threw up his hands when he saw his father and crowed lustily.

'Well, so you decided to come back and make it up to me before . . .' Clara began, and stopped. Her lips parted and she stared at Johnny a moment, then she asked, 'What is it, darling?'

'You heard the fire bell?' he asked.

She nodded. 'I ran out into the street, but I couldn't see any smoke.'

'There wasn't any fire,' he said, 'but we've got a pile of trouble heading our way.'

He hesitated, thinking that the problems he and Clara faced were nothing compared to the sudden threat of violence that endangered them now. He glanced around the room, at the happy baby in the high chair, the table with its red and white oil cloth covering, the stove with the pan of pudding and Clara standing beside it looking at him and waiting to hear what had happened.

'What is it?' Clara asked.

Johnny wiped a hand across his face. It came away wet. He was frightened, more frightened than he had ever been in his life. He felt his heart pounding, and now he could see his baby clubbed to death by these men, Clara raped with most of her clothes torn off her round, young body and this house a pile of smoking ashes.

He wasn't afraid of the fight that was shaping up. He'd managed to do his share in plenty of fights, and it wasn't just the chance that he might get killed, either. It was Clara and the baby and this house with the few bits of furniture they had gathered and their clothes destroyed and the keepsakes that could never be replaced.

Baldy Mack and young Chuck Morgan and Johnny Roan: three of them against a gang of hardcases, and not one of the three the kind of fighing man this job called for. It was too much, he told himself.

He was a fool. He'd take Billy and Clara out of town and then come back and help fight. He knew at once he could not. He might not get back in time. He would be no better than Limpy Smith and Elsie Mills if he did.

Clara came to him and shook him. 'Johnny, what is it?' She smelled her pudding burning and whirled and ran back to the stove and set the pan on the warming oven.

'A gang of outlaws moved in on the Morgan place early this morning,' he said. 'They shot and killed Chuck's grandpa. Chuck got to town and told us they're coming in at noon to rob the bank. Carl Sturtz has gone for help, but he may not get here in time. We figured on holing up in the jail all day so they can't kill us.'

Clara faced him, her eyes wide with horror, then she cried, 'No, Johnny. I'd be safer to stay here with Billy. Let them rob the bank. No use of you getting killed trying to save Jake Warner's money.'

He should have known she would take that attitude. He said, 'It's not just Jake Warner's money. It's money that belongs to everybody in town and some of the ranchers around here. I can't let them take it and you can't stay here. Sturtz knows these men. He says they're killers. They may burn the town and rape all the women they can find and kill the men just for the fun of killing. I thought about taking you out of town, but I didn't know where to take you.'

'There isn't any place to go unless we went clear into Douglas,' she said.

He nodded, 'That's what I decided. These men may stop at a ranch and if they found you there, it would be the end of you. We don't know what's safe and what isn't, and we sure can't guess the direction they'll go from here.

They'll want horses and they won't find many they can use in Sturtz's stable, so they'll probably stop at several ranches before they get out of the country. I guess the safest thing is to go to the jail with the rest of us, but it'll be a hot miserable day for you and Billy.'

'Who are the rest?' Clara asked.

'The Macks, Chuck, and Betsy,' he answered. 'Limpy Smith figured to get rich selling whisky to the outlaws, and that gave Elsie Mills the idea of selling them hot dinners. They'll both get killed before the day's over, but they wouldn't listen.'

'Six of us,' Clara whispered. 'Seven with Billy.'

'And only three men,' he said, 'but the outlaws won't be able to break into the jail. They can't knock down the stone walls and the door's solid. I think it's the best place. Let's pick up what Billy will need and get to the jail as soon as we can. Those men might not wait until noon.'

She hesitated, glancing around the room just as Johnny had a few minutes before, then she nodded and ran into their bedroom, calling back, 'Change Billy, will you?'

They worked feverishly for half an hour, filling two baskets with clothes and food for the baby. Johnny told her that Betsy and Mrs. Mack were taking food into the jail. Clara spooned as much of the pudding as she could get into a quart jar and screwed on a lid.

When they were ready to leave, she asked, 'Are you taking your guns?'

He had not intended to, knowing that Baldy Mack would move the guns from the store to the jail, then he realized that the outlaws would probably search the houses for guns and ammunition and he would be foolish to leave anything here they could use.

He nodded. 'I'd better.'

He found an empty flour sack in the bedroom and dropped all of his shells into it, then picked up his gun belt and buckled it around his waist. He left the room with the sack of shells, pulled his Winchester and shotgun off the antler rack in the front room and took the baby from Clara.

Now he was suddenly filled with a desperate need to hurry, reminding himself again that the outlaws might not wait until noon. The money still had to be carried from the bank to the jail. He jerked his head at Clara—'Let's get moving.'

She nodded and, picking up the two baskets, followed him out of the house into the hot sunshine. He walked fast, holding the baby against his shoulder with his right arm. Clara ran to keep up. Then he remembered about Elsie Mills and told Clara. It seemed so ludicrous and unreal that he began to laugh, then forced himself to stop as he realized he was almost hysterical.

He took a long breath and slowed up, aware

that Clara was having to run to keep up with him. He said, 'I couldn't help thinking when I was coming to the house awhile ago that I'd done one good thing. But butting heads with Elsie Mills, I fixed it so you never could work for her again. She'll never forgive me, so she won't want you around her.'

'I don't think that's funny,' Clara said. 'If something happens to you, I may have to work for her.'

'Never,' Johnny said. 'You and Billy had better starve first. She's the worst bitch I ever ran into. Imagine trying to make Betsy go back to the Bon Ton with her.'

'I can imagine it all right,' Clara said. 'Don't forget I have worked for her.'

They were almost to the jail now. He shot a glance at Clara, realizing he had never given a thought to what she had been through during the months before they were married. Working for Elsie Mills would be strictly hell.

When they reached the jail, they found the interior thick with dust. Betsy had just finished sweeping. She stood outside the door, coughing, her broom leaning against the stone wall. As soon as she got over her coughing spell, she took the baby and began talking to him. Mrs. Mack hurried past them and went inside with an armload of cans of food and came out immediately and sneezed.

'My goodness, Betsy,' Mrs. Mack said. 'I didn't think you could find that much dust in town.'

Betsy giggled. 'I didn't, either, but I found out there was. I guess I even got some on my face. Chuck told me I needed to wash.'

'A little dust won't hurt the looks of a pretty girl,' Johnny said as he emptied his flour sack on the ground beside the door. 'I'll get the money from the bank.' He glanced along the road that led west out of town toward the Morgan place. 'Nothing in sight yet.'

'No,' Betsy said. 'I've been watching, too.'

Johnny had leaned his Winchester and shotgun against the wall. 'I'll be back in a little while,' he said.

'We'll be all right,' Clara told him. 'Billy always did take to Betsy. We'll go inside as soon as the dust settles.'

'That bake oven in there will upset Billy,' Betsy said. 'I don't believe it's cooled off for a week, and the next hot day just makes it a little hotter.'

Johnny ran to the bank, the sense of urgency driving him harder than ever. It was still a long time until noon, but there would be no time to relax until everything was inside the jail. He unlocked the front door of the bank and went inside.

The interior of the frame building was hot. It had been hot yesterday and the day before yesterday, but still he had worn his suit and white shirt and tie. He wondered with growing irritation what Jake Warner was wearing in

Douglas.

He took only a few minutes to unlock the big safe and drop the bags of gold and silver coins into the flour sack, then the stack of greenbacks. He shoved the heavy door of the safe back into place and emptied the drawers of the teller's cage of both coins and paper money.

He spilled half a dozen silver dollars that jingled as they struck the floor and rolled away until they hit the wall. It wasn't worth the few seconds time it would take to pick them up, he thought, and ran out of the bank, leaving the door unlocked behind him.

He wondered what Black Jack and his bunch would think when they found no money except the silver dollars on the floor, then he laughed, a humorless laugh because he was thinking of Jake Warner who would demand to know why he hadn't taken the time to pick up the silver dollars. Chances were the old tight wad would take it out of this month's salary.

He saw that Baldy Mack and Chuck Morgan had finished moving guns and ammunition and supplies from the store into the jail. The women were standing in the small spot of shade that fell into the street from the jail. Suddenly a startling question came to him. Could he trust everyone who had sought refuge in the jail, or would he have to keep his eyes on the sack of money all the time he was here?

CHAPTER SIX

After they had finished breakfast Black Jack took one of the two bunks in the Morgan shack, Cutter the other. The rest of the men went outside to sleep. In a matter of seconds Cutter had dropped off into the dreamless sleep of an exhausted man. Black Jack was just as tired as Cutter, but he didn't sleep . . . he wanted to sleep, but he couldn't . . . he couldn't even remember when he had really slept, the good kind of sleep that restores a tired man.

Black Jack had been tired mentally, emotionally, and physically for a long time. There had been a day when he thought he would not live to see another sunrise, but somehow he had survived the agony of the Yuma prison, an agony that a good many of his fellow prisoners had not survived. The only reason he was still alive was because he had sworn he would make people . . . a lot of people . . . pay for the suffering he had undergone.

Oh, it wouldn't be the same people, but what the hell difference did that make? Sure, he'd rather have squared accounts with the brutal guards who had beaten him and fed him thin soup and meat crawling with maggots, guards who had no sense of human decency and who had made him suffer every indignity their animal-like minds could think of.

But it wasn't just the prison and the guards. There had been his wife, his sweet, gentle, ever-loving wife who had run off with another man the year before his release. He didn't know where she was, but he wished he did. There was nothing in this world he wanted as much as he wanted to put his hands on her white, soft throat and squeeze until all life was gone.

It was a futile dream and he knew it. He simply had no idea where she was, but he was sure she had gone a long ways because she would know what he would do if he ever got his hands on her. He had made no effort to trace her; he knew he didn't have time. He couldn't get even with her, but he could make other women suffer; he couldn't get even with the guards who had tortured him, but he could make other men suffer, and he had.

Black Jack stared at the ceiling as the sun climbed higher into the sky and the heat grew worse until it was almost unbearable inside the cabin. Still Cutter kept on snoring and a big bluebottle fly kept buzzing as he bumped against a window glass. Black Jack wiped the sweat from his face and continued to stare at the ceiling.

He knew the kind of men he was leading; he knew exactly what he had to do to keep on leading them. There was no sense of loyalty to him in any of them except Cutter. They wanted three things: money, whisky, and women.

As long as the train and bank robberies he planned worked out and they took in the money to buy whisky and women, he was all right. The last caper had failed as far as money went. One more like it and he and Cutter would be all that was left of the gang, so they had to pull off a good job in Platte City.

Black Jack knew well enough that his own life wasn't worth much. The country behind was buzzing with law men. For the moment he had thrown them off the trail, but it was only a matter of a few days, or a week at most, when they'd close in on him. Too many Pinkertons and too many U.S. Marshals were on his trail. They weren't going to pass up a reward as big as the one that had been offered for him, dead or alive.

He almost laughed when he thought about it. He'd fooled them plenty so far. Once he got into the Colorado high country he'd fool them some more. He didn't really care about living. What he did care about was making the most of the days he still had left.

Dying quick and sudden wouldn't be so bad; dying slowly in the heat and filth and misery of Yuma had been another matter. He wasn't going back there or to the Colorado pen or anywhere else that he didn't want to go. From now on he would be either a free man or a dead one, and there were moments when he thought he preferred death to freedom.

It was almost time to start for Platte City. For a little while he thought about the women they would find; they would use them and kill them, they would kill the men and clean out the bank and be on their way in a few hours. His life would likely be a short one, but a life that Wyoming people would never forget.

He rose because it was just too hot to lie here inside the cabin any longer. It had been hotter in Yuma, but there had been nothing he could do about it. Now at least he didn't have to stay in any one place.

He crossed the room to the bench by the door, poured water into a wash pan from a bucket, and splashed the water over his face. He picked up the towel from a nail near the door and dried; he filled the dipper and drank some of it and spewed a mouthful on the floor. God, it was awful. He'd give anything for a cold drink. Once they got into the mountains he'd have one.

Black Jack glanced around, saw an oil can on the shelf back of the stove and, picking it up, jerked the potato off the spout and poured the coal onto the bunk where he had been lying. He struck a match and tossed it onto the bunk. When the flame leaped up, he grabbed the bucket and emptied the water on Cutter's face.

Cutter sat up, snorting and cursing and

wiping the water from his face. Black Jack yelled, 'Fire.' Cutter suddenly realized the other bunk was in flames. He let out a scared yip and grabbed his hat and lunged for the door.

Black Jack followed him outside, laughing as much as he could these days, a sort of sour, choppy laugh. He said, 'You almost got barbecued, Cutter.'

'You and your damned jokes,' Cutter snarled. 'Someday you'll think of one too many.'

Black Jack shrugged. 'Come on. Let's get our outfit into the saddle.'

Cutter glanced at the sun. 'It ain't noon yet.'

'Close enough,' Black Jack said. 'We're wasting time. Besides, whoever was in the cabin and got away may have spread the word, so we'd better move.'

The men were hard to waken, and when they finally were aroused enough to stagger to the horse trough, they were short-tempered and grouchy. Several of them including Billy Horn glanced at the sun and said it was too early.

Black Jack gave one answer. 'It'll be close to noon when we get there.'

By this time the cabin was a mass of flames. Billy Horn was the only real rebel in the bunch and Black Jack had known all the time that sooner or later he'd have to cut him down to size. Now Horn motioned to the cabin. 'What the hell, Jack? Do you have to burn every damned place you see?

Black Jack dropped his right hand to the butt of his gun and cuffed his hat back off his sweaty forehead with his thumb. He said, 'Horn, it just happens I like to start fires.'

'You like to kill people, too,' Horn said angrily. 'I don't see no sense in making people madder than they already are. As long as we go around killing and burning for no reason, that's what we're gonna do.'

Black Jack eased his gun out of leather. He asked, his voice deceptively soft, 'You got some objections maybe, Horn?'

Horn looked at the gun, then raised his eyes to Black Jack's dark ones. 'Not just now,' he said, and turned toward the corral.

Black Jack's gaze followed him, his gun still out of the holster. He was going to have to kill the bastard, but he'd wait. Billy was a good man with a gun, the best in the outfit. They might hit trouble in Platte City; they might need Horn, so it would be a waste to kill him now.

'Saddle up, all of you,' he shouted, and strode to the corral.

Within five minutes they were lined out toward Platte City, Black Jack and Cutter in the lead.

CHAPTER SEVEN

Carl Sturtz rode as hard as he could to Douglas, but it was later in the morning when he arrived than he had hoped it would be. The truth was he just couldn't stand the pounding of a saddle the way he had when he was young. Once more he was reminded that his good years were a long ways behind him.

He dismounted when he reached the gate that opened into the county fair grounds. The ticket seller was a Douglas business man he knew by name. He asked, 'Alec, is the sheriff here or down town?'

The Douglas man squinted against the morning sun and studied Sturtz, then he said sullenly, 'How the hell would I know?'

Sturtz thought he might as well expect this kind of treatment. Some of these Douglas people thought they owned the county and he, Carl Sturtz, was nothing but a stableman from somewhere out in the country and a has-been deputy. He said, 'Then I'll look.'

'Pay your way into the fair, damn it,' the ticket seller said harshly. 'Who do you think you are, somebody with special privileges maybe.'

'I'll pay you nothing,' Sturtz snapped. 'I'm a county official here on county business. If you want the price of a ticket, send your bill to the

45

county.'

Sturtz got back on his horse and dug in his spurs. The ticket seller started to step in front of him, his hand out, but Sturtz's horse barreled straight ahead. If the man hadn't reversed himself suddenly so that he lost his balance and sprawled into the dust, the horse would have stepped on him.

The man yelled, 'I'll get you fired for that.'

Sturtz didn't bother to say anything to him. He didn't slow up or stop until he reached the cattle barn. Seeing a hitch rack, he reined up and dismounted and tied. He began looking for the sheriff in the cattle barn, asking every man he met, but none of them had seen Newel that day.

He left the barn and spent an hour looking for the sheriff, a wasted hour, he thought bitterly, and found no trace of him. Several men admitted seeing Newel on the fair grounds yesterday afternoon, but not this morning.

He made the mistake of walking past the building that housed the sewing, cooking, and canned exhibits. His wife saw him and, knowing his aversion for fairs, ran outside and asked, 'Carl, what are you doing here?'

He had no intention of telling her what was going to happen in Platte City. She'd carry on about not wanting him to get killed because they had no children and who would take care of her if he was murdered; he had no business being a law man at his age because he would get killed if he kept on wearing the star. He'd sure heard this over and over and he was damned if he was going to listen to any more of it.

Sturtz started to say he was looking for the sheriff and knew that would lead to more argument and more demands for an explanation, so he lied to her. He said, 'I'm looking for Jake Warner.'

'Oh, he's inside,' Mrs. Sturtz said. 'I saw him walking by while ago and I wanted him to admire my afghan. I hoped he'd pay me to make him one.' She whirled toward the door and called, 'Mr. Warner. Oh, Mr. Warner.'

Sturtz groaned. Sometimes he wondered how he could possibly keep jumping from the frying pan into the fire the way he did with his wife, but he succeeded in doing exactly that when he had no intention of doing anything of the kind.

There was nothing to do but wait and think up a lie to tell the banker, but a moment later Jake Warner came out of the building and stared at him expectantly. He had not been able to think of an adequate lie in that short time, so he told the truth.

'An outlaw gang murdered Bucky Morgan this morning.' Sturtz blurted, 'and they're coming to Platte City to rob your bank at noon.'

The old man stared at Sturtz for several

seconds before he fully comprehended what the deputy had said, then his face turned pale and he backed up to lean against the wall. He put his hand over his heart and began to tremble as he moaned, 'Oh, my God! My God.'

'Johnny Roan's going to move your money into the jail,' Sturtz said quickly. 'Everybody that's left in town will go into the jail and keep it locked until I get there with help. That's why I'm looking for the sheriff.'

Warner put out a shaking hand as if to thrust back the possibility that the bank would be robbed. 'Somebody will steal the money if he does that. He's got to keep it locked up in the safe. He's got a gun. He can keep them from getting the money.'

'Jake, are you paying Johnny Roan enough to have him risk his life defending your bank?' Sturtz demanded.

He liked young Johnny Roan and he had never liked Jake Warner. The banker's attitude turned his stomach. If Warner were back there in Platte City he wouldn't risk his neck a minute, but he could stand here where he was perfectly safe and claim that Johnny Roan who had a wife and baby ought to fight to protect his money.

'Carl, that's no way to talk to Mr. Warner,' Mrs. Sturtz cried, horrified. 'Have you forgotten who he . . .'

'Oh hell,' Sturtz said angrily, and turned on

48

his heel.

He strode toward his horse, knowing that he'd have to go to the business section of town to find Newel. He'd probably be in a bar and he'd probably be drunk or well on the road to getting drunk. The last thing Abe Newel would want to do would be to ride to Platte City with a whacking headache and Sturtz guessed he'd have one.

He had reached his horse and had mounted when he heard Warner call, 'Wait, Sturtz. Wait a minute.'

He waited, swearing under his breath. It seemed that everything was conspiring to make him waste time. He didn't know when the outlaws would reach Platte City; he didn't know how long the handful of people in the jail could stand it, cooped up inside it and knowing all the time that if they tossed the money out, Black Jack and his men would take it and probably ride out of town.

'You'll find the sheriff in the hotel bar,' Warner said. 'I think you will anyhow. I was with him last night playing poker. We had a big game going and I suppose they're still at it.'

Sturtz groaned. 'He won't want to leave town.'

'You go see him,' Warner said, his voice trembling. 'I'll find a horse and buggy or something and I'll be there as soon as I can. If you can't talk him into going with you, maybe I can.'

'All right,' Sturtz agreed. 'You get there as fast as you can. You're a bigger tax payer than I am, so he might listen to you.'

Sturtz touched up his horse. As he rode through the gate, the ticket seller stepped back, cursing him as he rode by. He felt like stopping and knocking a few teeth down the man's throat, but he couldn't take time to indulge in a personal row.

He thought about that as he rode toward the business block. It had been a long time since he'd let his temper crowd him the way it was crowding him now. He guessed that his age hadn't taken all of his gumption.

There was a lot to the old saying about a man being as old as he felt. The next time his wife said anything to him about being old, he'd give her the back of his hand. What he really needed was a young wife, a girl like Betsy Mills. Maybe he'd get one if he had to go on listening to her remarks.

Dismounting in front of the hotel, he went inside. Traffic was beginning to flow along Main Street toward the fair grounds. In another hour the place would be jumping. The lobby was crowded with cowboys and ranchers and a few wives, and when he finally had bulled his way into the bar, he saw it was even more crowded.

'Where'll I find the sheriff?' Sturtz asked one of the bartenders.

The man finished pouring a drink, stared at

Sturtz a moment, and shrugged. 'I dunno,' he said.

The red flag of sheer madness began waving in front of Sturtz. He leaned across the bar and grabbed a handful of the bartender's white shirt. 'By God,' he said, 'I'm getting tired of being put off. This is official business. Where is he?'

For a moment the bartender hesitated, then motioned toward the back room and shrugged again. 'He's in a poker game. Now let go of me.'

Sturtz released his grip and, wheeling away from the bar, fought his way through the crowd to the door of the back room. He opened it and went in. Several men were crowded around a big, green-topped table, others were standing behind them watching. Sturtz recognized most of them, ranchers and Douglas business men. Newel was there, his stubble-covered face flushed, tobacco smoke making a heavy blue cloud above the table.

'Sheriff,' Sturtz said, 'we need you in Platte City. The bank is going to be robbed.'

The sheriff glanced at him, then motioned to two men standing behind him. 'Hogwash,' he said. 'Throw him out.'

The men were young and strong, and before Sturtz realized what was happening, he was propelled through the door into the saloon, the door was shut behind him, and he was standing there, staring dazedly at it.

51

He wondered why people put up with a sheriff like Abe Newel. Then he thought: *Why don't I run for sheriff this fall?*

CHAPTER EIGHT

Johnny Roan stood beside his wife in front of the jail, his gaze turning to the west to follow the road that led to town from the Morgan place. He would then glance at the sun, guess the time, and turn to look at Clara and the baby. A few seconds later he would glance back along the road again. This was the way it had been for about two hours, the slowest two hours he had ever spent in his life.

Everything was in the jail that they intended to move. They had agreed they'd better get inside and bar the heavy door, but still they lingered out here in front simply because they shrank from shutting themselves inside the jail until they had to.

The dust that Betsy had stirred up when she'd swept had settled a long time, but the heat had increased until it was enough to make them wonder if they could stand being cooped up inside with the door closed. Most of the morning had been unusually still with no hint of a wind, just the steady glare of the sun and the decreasing patch of shade in front of the building as the sun had risen higher into the sky.

Chuck Morgan and Betsy had moved away from the others; now they stood holding hands at the front east corner of the jail, their heads close together as they talked in low tones. Johnny felt sorry for them, sorry because Chuck had lost his grandfather, the only relative he had, and sorry because Betsy was Elsie Mill's daughter. It was a tough proposition to be in love at that age, with no job and no prospects of one.

Baldy Mack kept wiping his face with a red bandanna as he glanced at his wife, then he'd look away from her. Johnny, watching him, sensed that he was close to panic. Mack was trembling, the pulse at his temples was pounding as if the blood was about to break through the arteries.

Mrs. Mack seemed unconcerned about what was going to happen, but it occurred to Johnny that the storekeeper was more wind than anything else. When the showdown came, Mack wasn't going to be worth much.

It was just as Baldy Mack had said earlier that morning. You never knew about a man until you get into a squeeze, Johnny thought bleakly. Mack had probably not even known about himself. In the end Chuck Morgan who was still a boy would stack up higher than Mack.

Johnny remembered talking to Carl Sturtz about it once, and Sturtz had said you couldn't tell how a man would measure up until he had been tested. Sometimes a man you thought you could bank on the most would cave in when the shooting started, and another man you had overlooked would come through. Sturtz knew from experience, but it seemed queer that Baldy Mack would say almost the same thing, and then be the first one to fold.

Johnny was pleasantly surprised by Clara. She wasn't worrying now. Not about the danger from Black Jack's gang of outlaws anyhow. Her worry was about the baby. Would he be able to stand the heat if they had to stay inside the rest of the day? He could if he had to, Johnny thought, but a crying baby was hard on everybody's nerves.

Johnny was the first to notice the dust several minutes before the riders could be seen. It was then about eleven. He waited as long as he thought he could, then he said, 'They're coming. We'd better get inside.'

Baldy Mack gave a start and whirled toward the corner of the building where Chuck and Betsy stood. Mrs. Mack must have expected this. She grabbed him by the arm as she said, 'Looks to me like Johnny's the general. We'll do what he says.'

Johnny knew then, knew as certainly as if Baldy Mack had told him in words. The storekeeper would have run away if he could. Betsy and Chuck moved quickly to the door as Mrs. Mack led her husband inside. Chuck shot a glance at Johnny who waited until the others were through the door.

'He was fixing to run out on us, wasn't he?' Chuck asked in a low voice. 'That bastard's full of talk, but he ain't no better'n Limpy Smith.'

'I wouldn't say that,' Johnny said. 'At least he's not out trying to sell merchandise to Black Jack.' He shut the door and dropped the heavy bar, then turned to the others. 'Take the loophole next to the door, Chuck. Baldy, get the one in the corner.'

Mack picked up a rifle and stood facing Johnny until his wife took his arm. 'Come on, Baldy.' Still he stood there, staring vacantly at Johnny, saliva drooling from the corners of his mouth. His wife slapped him on the cheek. 'Come out of it, Baldy. You've got a job of fighting to do today.'

He shook his head after she slapped him and let her lead him to the far loophole. Johnny said. 'Clara, you and Betsy get over yonder in the corner next to me. Stay there. If we have any shooting, you'll be safe. We'll get some bullets through the windows, but I doubt that any are going to make it through the door.'

He picked up his rifle, wishing they had shutters for the two windows that were on the street side. There had been danger from raiding bands of Sioux and Cheyennes when the jail was built. Its original purpose had been more as a fort than a jail. That was the reason for the loopholes, and Johnny guessed that shutters as heavy as the door had been stored somewhere in the jail at that time, but he had no idea where they were, or even if they were still in existence.

The baby had gone to sleep in Clara's arms, and now she laid him on a pallet made from quilts she had brought from the house. His little face was shiny with beads of perspiration, but he was sleeping peacefully enough.

Betsy sat down on the floor, her back to the wall. She smiled at Clara who sat between her and the baby. She asked, 'Scared?'

'A little.' Clara smiled back. 'But we'll be all right. I know we will.'

'So do I.' Betsy looked at Chuck, and said in a low voice, 'Clara, you weren't much older than I am when you and Johnny were married, and he wasn't any older than Chuck. Have you ever been sorry you got married when you did?'

Johnny was still at the window, but he heard what the girl asked. He glanced quickly at Clara, wondering what she would say, and as quickly glanced away. He guessed he was not supposed to listen, but apparently Clara wanted him to hear. She said louder than she needed to, 'No, Betsy. I have never been sorry. Not for one little minute.'

Johnny moved from the window to the loophole because the outlaw band was just riding into town. He said, 'Thank you, Mrs.

Roan.'

'You are most welcome, Mr. Roan.' Clara said as Betsy giggled.

'No shooting,' Johnny called. 'We don't want to let them know we're here until we have to.'

Chuck nodded and Baldy Mack, standing at the loophole because his wife was close beside him, stared blankly at Johnny as if he didn't even hear what had been said. The whisper of hoofs dropping into the street dust came to Johnny as he peered through the loophole, the first of the outlaws just then riding past the front of the jail.

From the description Chuck had given, Johnny judged the leader of the gang, Black Jack, was the front rider. Very broad of shoulder and dark-complexioned, the outlaw had the appearance of a general, Johnny thought.

The skinny man who rode slightly behind him would be Cutter, a hideously ugly man with an eagle beak for a nose, and a mouth that was no more than a slit across the lower part of his face. He glanced at the jail when he came opposite, and Johnny found himself looking squarely at the man's face. He was shocked at his expression, particularly that thin, cruel mouth.

Black Jack and Cutter could be knocked out of their saddles now as easily as shooting pigeons off a barn roof. Johnny was tempted, then remembered the agreement with Carl Sturtz. He had come close to thumbing back the hammer of his Winchester. Then he heard the click of Chuck's rifle being cocked, and he realized what was in the boy's mind.

'Don't do it,' Johnny said in a low tone.

Chuck sighed and shook his head. 'Aw, I dunno, Johnny. That was the best chance we'll ever have to fill those two killers full of lead.'

'I know,' Johnny said. 'I had the same notion, but it's like Sturtz said. Maybe they won't find out we're here. When they see the money's gone from the bank, maybe they'll ride on out of town. If we start shooting, they'll know we're here and we'll have a fight. We'd best play it easy for a while.'

The rest of the wolf pack had ridden past now. Johnny was shocked. He had never seen a tougher, meaner, more brutal looking bunch of men in his life than these. That was exactly what Chuck had said. He realized that Carl Sturtz knew what he was talking about, and he told himself that Limpy Smith and Elsie Mills were as good as dead.

Johnny took a long, sighing breath. Sweat rolled down his cheeks and he jerked his handkerchief out of his pocket and wiped his face with it. The outlaws had pulled up in front of the bank, and several had gone inside. Now Johnny heard his own breathing; he felt his pulse pound in his veins. Up until this moment his worries and fears had been only in his mind. They were greater than that now. Ten men more animals than human had actually arrived in Platte City.

He turned to look at Clara, every nerve in his body humming as if each had been pulled tight on a winch. He had never seen her more attractive than she was at this moment or more desirable; he had never loved her as much as he did right now.

For no reason that was apparent to any of them, the baby woke up and began to cry, so loudly that it seemed to everyone in the jail that Black Jack and his men must have heard him. Clara snatched him up and held him against her breast, patting him on the back and comforting him, but the damage had been done, Johnny thought. The damage had been done.

CHAPTER NINE

Carl Sturtz was in a foul mood as he rammed his way through the crowd in the bar to the street door. He understood some things now he should have understood before. Abe Newel had given way to the pressure exerted by Jake Warner and Baldy Mack and the other businessmen in Platte City to appoint a local deputy, but Newel had never intended to support him or have him lift a finger to enforce the law.

That was it, Sturtz told himself angrily. Appointing him had been a form just to get the Platte City businessmen off his back. Newel, like a lot of other people, considered him a has-been and could be kicked around without any risk of being kicked back.

Well, by God, he wasn't a has-been, and before the day was over Abe Newel and a lot of other people would know it. With that thought, twenty years slid off Carl Sturtz's shoulders.

He had no more than cleared the door and stepped onto the boardwalk when he ran into Jake Warner. The banker's claw-like hands grabbed his arms. 'What did he say, Sturtz? Is he going to raise a posse to stop these men?'

Sturtz looked at Warner and thought of Abe Newel, half-drunk and playing poker while Jake Warner's bank was being robbed, and suddenly it occurred to him that there was a sort of queer, left-handed kind of justice here. Warner had supported Newel the last election, and now Newel was turning out to be exactly the kind of sheriff that Warner deserved.

'No,' Sturtz said. 'He wouldn't even listen to me. He's playing poker and he had a couple of his plug-uglies throw me out.'

Warner's mouth began to twitch. He swore, then suddenly he straightened up, his hands fisted, and he said, 'Let's go back and see him. He's got to protect my bank and I'm going to tell him so.'

Sturtz's first impulse was to say to hell with it, that he was going back to Platte City and take care of Black Jack and his gang by himself, but he decided that was stupid. One law man against ten outlaws was a bad gamble, and Newel just might pay attention to Jake Warner who could and often did control a number of Platte City votes.

Sturtz nodded. 'All right, Jake, and you'd better do some talking. I ain't of a mind to take any more kicking around.'

He wheeled and went back into the bar. Warner followed, close behind. Sturtz barreled his way through the crowd again, reached the back room and yanked the door open. He went in, Warner still only a step behind.

The sheriff looked up, saw who it was, and began to curse, his liquor-flushed face turning dark red with quick anger. 'Old man, if you've got to be roughed up to be taught a lesson, we can sure do it.' Newel motioned to the men who had thrown Sturtz out a few minutes before. 'Boys, I guess you'd better let my deputy know how it feels when you don't learn any better than he does.'

'You bet,' one of them said.

They were grinning as they started toward Sturtz, then they stopped flat-footed as Sturtz pulled his gun. He said, 'Newel, you keep those bastards coming at me and they'll get a snootful of lead.'

61

Warner had remained in the doorway. Now he walked to the table. He said bitterly, 'Abe, I helped you get elected. I've got a right to have protection for my bank. I insist on you taking a posse to Platte City and doing everything in your power to save my bank.'

Apparently Newel had not seen Warner until that moment, or at least had not recognized him. He did now. He folded his hand and laid it face down on the table. 'You sure do, Jake,' he said. 'Now just what is it I'm supposed to protect you from?'

'Tell him, Sturtz,' Warner said.

Sturtz told him, emphasizing that time was running out and if the outlaws weren't in Platte City right now, they soon would be. When he finished, Newel laughed. 'So that's it. Now who did you say was running that outfit?'

'Black Jack Connor, the bank robber,' Sturtz said. 'I know he's been in the Yuma pen, so he's either been released or he broke out. He's a bad actor.'

'He's a bad actor, all right,' Newel said, still amused by this. 'You say his old pal Cutter is with him?'

'That's what Chuck Morgan told us,' Sturtz said.

'Well sir, you have been taken,' Newel said. 'I guess that the Morgan kid needed some excitement. Maybe he wanted to look big to his girl. He's got a girl, ain't he?'

'Yeah,' Sturtz said. 'Betsy Mills.' His heart

was pumping hard now because he could see exactly what Newel was aiming at. 'I reckon you're wrong about me being taken. I heard what the boy said. I believe him.'

'You're a fool.' Newel slammed a big palm down against the table. 'I don't know about Cutter, but Black Jack is still in the Yuma pen. You ever hear of a man breaking out of there?'

'No, but . . .'

'All right.' Newel picked up his cards. 'Go on back to Platte City and tell that bunch of sheep they're all scared over a kid's wild tale that he made up. Jake, you go to the fair and forget it. Enjoy yourself.'

Warner didn't know what to believe, his gaze swinging back and forth between Newel and Sturtz. One of the poker players, impatient at the delay, said, 'Get 'em out of here, Abe. I figure you kicked up all this dust just to stop the game and change your luck.'

'I need it changed, all right,' Newel said, 'but this ain't my way of changing it.' He motioned to the door. 'Get along, Sturtz. I'm sorry he got you all excited this way, Jake, but you get a kid worked up and an old man wanting to attract a little attention, and this is the kind of trick they'll think of every time.'

'Newel,' Sturtz said, 'I don't know why the people of this county put up with a sheriff like you. I think I'll run against you in November so they'll have some kind of a choice.'

'You? Run against me?' Newel threw his big

head back and bellowed a laugh. 'You can vote for yourself, I guess. That'll be the only one you'll get.'

The rest of them were laughing, too, and Sturtz wished he hadn't said it. He eased toward the door, his gaze on the two men who had thrown him out. If they had pushed him, he would have shot both of them. In a way he wished they had. He was about ready to shoot them and Abe Newel, too.

This whole thing was illogical. For Newel to sit there and dismiss everything he had been told did not make sense, but Sturtz had heard stories like this about him. He had not believed them before. He did now, and he was convinced that if enough of these things had happened, the voters would throw him out if they had anybody else to vote for. All that Sturtz needed was one big performance to get a reputation. Taking Black Jack would do it.

Newel had picked up his cards and was calling for two more. Nobody around the table was paying any attention to either Sturtz or Warner. Sturtz left the room and forced his way through the crowd once more. When he reached the street, he saw that Warner was right behind him.

'I'll get back to Platte City.' Sturtz glanced at the sun. It was close to noon. 'I may be too late, but I'll do all I can to save your bank.'

Warner was scratching his chin, trying to believe what Newel had said, but having a little trouble with it. He said, 'I guess the sheriff would have heard it if a notorious outlaw like Black Jack had broken out of Yuma.'

'I don't think he broke out,' Sturtz said. 'It's more likely his term was up and he was released. He was sentenced to five years for bank robbery if I remember right, and he's been in there just about that long.'

'Newel still would have heard, wouldn't he?' Warner asked doggedly.

'Maybe not,' Sturtz said. 'You saw how he performed. He didn't give a damn about you or Platte City or your bank. He just wanted to go on playing poker.'

Sturtz untied his horse and mounted. Warner stepped off the boardwalk into the dust of the street, still wanting to believe Newel, but not fully able to. He said, 'When you get there, you tell Johnny to put that money back into the bank safe. Tell him I'll fire him if he don't do it.'

'I've got an idea you won't be firing him,' Sturtz said. 'He's too good a man to work for you. If I'm elected this fall, I might appoint him my deputy.'

'You couldn't beat Newel,' Warner said.

Sturtz leaned forward over the saddle horn. 'Jake, is this the first time you have heard of Newel being too drunk or too interested in playing poker or in his whoring around to attend to his job?'

'No,' the banker agreed reluctantly. 'It's

65

not.'

'What will it do for his reputation when everybody in the county hears that you would have been cleaned out if it hadn't been for me?' Sturtz asked.

He didn't wait for an answer. He whirled his horse and galloped down the street. His wife was just leaving the fair grounds. He groaned when he saw her motion to him, knowing he had neither the time nor the energy to argue with her, so he swung into an alley, not turning back into the Platte City road until he knew he was well past her.

He almost laughed aloud when he thought about what she would say when he told her he was going to run for sheriff, Well, he could handle one term at least if he had a good deputy to do the hard riding. Right now all he had to do was to figure out how to capture Black Jack and the nine members of his gang.

It could be done, he told himself as he rode back to Platte City, the sun beating down at him with its dry, wilting heat. It had been done. All he had to do was figure out how to do it this time.

CHAPTER TEN

Black Jack Connor found Platte City to be exactly what he had expected, small and run-down, with nearly every building on Main Street needing a coat of paint. No one was in sight on the street.

Two dominick hens scratched industriously in the archway of the livery stable and a gray, short-haired dog of questionable ancestry dozed in the sunshine in front of the saloon. A disreputable-looking tomcat with one ear missing sat on the sidewalk staring at the dog as if waiting for him to wake up so he could be challenged.

Black Jack's lips twisted into a humorless grin. It would be hell to live in a town like this, almost as much hell as he'd experienced in the Yuma pen. The difference was that he'd had physical walls around him and he'd had to stay; here the walls were invisible and people stayed because they lacked the gumption to leave.

For a moment Black Jack was afraid. He had a terrifying hunch that there would be nothing in this town worth having, not even a woman. If they found little or no money in the safe, he was in big trouble.

He could handle it, all right. He had always been able to handle trouble, but he didn't want trouble with his men. He wanted trouble with the good, self-righteous people of the town. There wouldn't be many in town today, but there would be a few, and he'd find them.

He glanced briefly at Cutter Doon's ugly face, wondering if the same notion had occurred to him. It would certainly be in Billy

Horn's head. He could be sure of that. Well, he'd take care of Billy Horn, but not until he had found out who was still in town.

Black Jack looked curiously at the stone jail, noting the loopholes and guessing that it had been built in Indian days when raiding bands of Sioux and Cheyennes were a constant threat. It would be a good place to hole up. If the townspeople had been warned, that was probably where they were.

He couldn't see any sign of life in the jail, but that proved nothing. If they were there, he'd probably take his bunch on out of town without getting his hands on the money or the townspeople. It would take an army to break into the jail.

Then he knew immediately he would not, could not, leave town without the money, not after missing out on the train robbery. He wouldn't risk his men's lives attacking the jail, even if they were willing which he knew they wouldn't be. But there was always an answer to a problem like this. It was up to him to find it. He was sure of one thing. If the safe in the bank was empty, he had to get into the jail. It was the next best bet.

He saw the bank ahead of him and reined toward it. He didn't hurry. If people were still in town, he didn't want them alarmed. Not yet. He dismounted as his men pulled up and stepped down a few seconds after he did.

Four men held the horses as he walked

toward the bank, Cutter Doon following him, then Billy Horn, and finally three others. The organization had been worked out weeks ago; every man knew exactly what he was to do, so now there was no hesitation and no indecision.

Black Jack was inside the bank and halfway to the cashier's window before he realized that the situation was as bad as he had feared. No one was in the room, the safe was open, and half a dozen silver dollars were scattered on the floor in front of the safe.

He knew, then, what had happened. He guessed he had actually expected it or he wouldn't have thought of the money being in the old jail. Someone had been in the hen house and had got away and had warned the townspeople. He didn't know how and it wasn't important. The important point was that it had been done and the money was gone.

Cutter Doon began to curse and Billy Horn, sizing up the situation a moment after Doon did, said harshly, 'You done it again, Connor. We're getting a big fat nothing.' He saw a silver dollar on the floor in front of him and kicked it across the room, adding savagely, 'A big fat nothing. That's what all of your schemes amount to.'

For a moment Black Jack fought his temper. He felt an almost uncontrollable urge to pull his gun as he wheeled toward Horn. He wanted to smoke him down more than he had wanted anything since leaving the Yuma

69

prison, but there was still a chance he'd need the man. The settlement with Horn could wait.

'Take a look in the safe, Cutter,' Black Jack said, ignoring Horn.

Quickly he pushed through the gate at the end of the counter and strode across the room to the office in the back. No one was there. The office looked as if it had not been used for several days. He ran his fingers through the dust on the desk top, curious about the reason for the office not being used, then he shrugged and crossed the room to the back door which opened onto a weed-covered alley. Nothing out here. He shut the door and hurried back to where the others waited, all but Cutter Doon staring at him with ill-concealed hostility.

'The money's still in town,' Black Jack said. 'Whoever runs this bank is still in town and he knows where the money is. We'll find him. Come on.'

He led the way out of the bank, and when they reached the horse holders, he said, 'The dinero's been taken out of the safe and hidden. We'll find the people and then we'll find the money. You boys put the horses in the livery stable and feed and water 'em. See if there are any horses in the stable we can use. Come to the saloon as soon as you're done with the horses. Use the alley door. I don't want to lose any of you in case they're holed up somewhere along the street and decide to cut loose.'

'I figure they're yonder in that old stone jail,' Cutter Doon said. 'I thought about it when we rode past while ago. Chances are they've got rifles and they're lined on us right now.'

'Don't act as if you're guessing that,' Black Jack warned. 'We'll mosey around like we don't know where they are. We'll cut the dust out of our throats and figure out what to do.'

'Mind telling me what makes you so damned smart?' Billy Horn demanded. 'You know they're holed up in the jail and they've got the dinero over there with 'em. Seems to me that's knowing a hell of a lot for a man who just rode into town.'

'It's logical, ain't it?' Black Jack asked.

'Supposing you're right,' Billy said. 'How are you figuring on getting the dinero?'

They had paused in the street in front of the saloon. Now Black Jack wheeled away from the others and pushed through the batwings. He had no answer to that question and Billy Horn knew it. It graveled him that a young punk like Horn could see through him better than any of the old timers in the outfit.

Just as the batwings slapped shut behind him, Billy Horn grabbed an arm. 'By God, Connor,' Horn said between clenched teeth, 'you're gonna answer my questions or I'll . . .'

'No you won't,' Black Jack said, jerking free. 'I'll answer your questions, but it'll take a little time. If you keep pushing, we'll be shooting each other and that ain't why we're here. We can do that any time.'

Horn let him go, scowling as if thinking about Black Jack's words. Cutter Doon, coming behind Black Jack and Horn, heard what had been said. He caught up with Horn and caught his shoulder. He said softly, 'Wait.' Horn stopped and turned to face him. He said, 'Billy, you've been bucking for trouble for a long time. You're gonna get it, but why don't you wait for it instead of pushing?'

Horn nodded. 'I reckon the time will come without me pushing.'

Black Jack had gone straight to the bar, surprised to see a man wearing an apron waiting there for them. The bartender called amiably, 'Welcome to Platte City, gents. What'll it be?'

'Whisky,' Black Jack said. 'We've come a long ways and we're thirsty and tired and mean. You give us any of your belly-wash and I'll personally skin you alive.'

'Yes sir,' the bartender said. 'I wouldn't serve belly-wash to men like you. No sir. This is the best.'

Cutter Doon stood beside Black Jack, Billy Horn and the other three lining up between Doon and the end of the bar.

'I'm Limpy Smith,' the barman said as he poured the drinks. 'I own the place. We ain't been real busy the last few days with the fair running in Douglas, so I'm glad to see you

72

boys.'

'You won't be after you get to know us,' Black Jack said. 'We rode into town to clean out the bank, but the safe's empty. Seeing as we didn't find no dinero, we may take it out of your hide.'

Limpy Smith blinked and rubbed a hand across his mouth, his face turning pale. He said, 'Well sir, my hide ain't worth much, but I might be worth quite a bit to you alive.'

Black Jack picked his glass up, gulped his drink, and then set the glass down. He leaned forward so he could see Billy Horn standing along the bar to his right. He said, 'I can answer one of your questions now. We've got a key that'll open the jail if the people are in there.'

'I don't see no key,' Billy said. 'You're bulling us again.'

'No.' Black Jack nodded at Limpy. 'This is an important man in the community. If we march him out of here with a gun in his back, they'll open the jail and throw the money out.'

Billy Horn snorted. 'The hell they will.'

'You just heard him say he was worth quite a bit to us alive.' Black Jack turned to Smith again. 'How did you get word we were coming into town?'

'There was a kid at the Morgan place where you killed the old man,' Smith answered. 'He was in the hen house watching when you done it. He slipped out and crawled along an

73

irrigation ditch and ran into town.'

'Where is everybody?'

'In the jail,' Smith answered. 'Everybody but me and Elsie Mills. She's in the café. She figured you'd want a hot meal while you're here. I figured you'd want some drinks. That's why we didn't stay with the others.'

Black Jack leaned forward again to look at Billy Horn. 'It'll work, all right. We've got two hostages. Them folks in the jail will open up to save their lives. They'll do it for a woman if they won't do it for him.' He jabbed a forefinger at Smith. 'How about it? You reckon we'll get the money in exchange for you and this woman you mentioned?'

'No sense killing us,' Smith blurted. 'We stayed out of the jail just so we could wait on you and your men. Wouldn't be right to kill us.'

'No, it wouldn't for a fact,' Black Jack admitted, 'but you see, I ain't done nothing that was right for a long time. Now tell me about the bank money? Did they take it with 'em into the jail like I guessed?'

Limpy Smith nodded sullenly. 'Yeah, it's there.'

'How many are in the jail?'

'Seven, including a baby.'

'Who are they?'

'The kid that fetched the warning. Chuck Morgan's his name. Elsie Mills's daughter Betsy is there. A couple that own the store

74

named Mack. Then there's the young couple named Roan. They're the ones with the baby. Johnny Roan's the one who works in the bank and moved the money into the jail.'

The four men who had taken care of the horses came into the saloon from the alley. Black Jack said, 'Serve these men their drinks.' He wheeled away from the bar and shouldered through the batwings. He shouted from the sidewalk in front of the saloon, 'You hear me, you people in the jail?'

No answer. Black Jack waited a moment, then he said, 'I reckon you can hear me, all right. Now you listen good. We're here to rob the bank and we ain't leaving town till we've got the dinero that was in the safe. You fetch it to us and we'll ride out of town and nobody gets hurt. If you don't, we'll shoot your friend Smith.'

Still no answer. Irritated, Black Jack yelled, 'Damn it, you'd better do what you're told. We're gonna have a drink or two and eat dinner. I'll give you an hour to think it over. If you haven't given us the dinero by that time, Smith is a dead man.'

He wheeled back into the saloon, irritation growing in him because he had expected some kind of answer from the people in the jail. The silence puzzled him.

'You were taking a chance, standing out there like you were,' Cutter Doon said. 'They could have drilled you from the jail real easy.'

Black Jack shook his head. 'Naw. They were worrying too much about our bartender to shoot me.'

Smith's face was shiny with sweat. He said, his voice trembling, 'You shouldn't make threats like that. You won't shoot me. You've got no reason to.'

'You're dead wrong, mister,' Billy Horn said. 'Black Jack Connor has killed at least five men he had no reason to. I'd say you were Number Six.'

Black Jack picked up the bottle and filled his glass. He said, 'That's right. We'll put it on your tombstone. Number Six sent to hell by Black Jack Connor.'

CHAPTER ELEVEN

The Roan baby stopped crying and sniffled a moment, then dropped off to sleep again. Every adult in the jail held his or her breath, thinking the outlaw pack must certainly have heard the baby's crying, but apparently none of them had. The men who had been in the bank came back into the street. There was some talk, then the horse holders led the horses to the livery stable and the others went into the saloon.

Johnny Roan took his handkerchief out of his pocket and wiped his face again. It seemed to him that the temperature was going up every minute. He looked at Clara and tried to smile, but it was a sorry effort. The interior of the jail would indeed be an oven before sundown.

He wasn't sure how long they could stand it any more than he knew when the outlaws would leave town. Now that their course had been decided and they were stuck here inside the jail, he wondered if he had done right. Maybe he should have taken a horse and buggy from the livery stable and moved his family to Douglas. The money, too.

He had a guilty conscience as he glanced at Clara and the baby and turned his gaze away. Maybe he had been more concerned about the money than he had been the safety of his wife and baby.

Betsy Mills sneezed and giggled as she said something to Chuck Morgan. Johnny didn't worry about the outlaws hearing the sneeze. If they hadn't heard the baby, they wouldn't hear the girl. There would be more sneezes before the day was over. The dust that had been raised early that morning when the jail was swept out had settled, but still there was dust in the air and it seemed to Johnny that every time someone moved it raised a new cloud of dust. At least the smell and taste of it were constant.

No one said anything for a time except the whispered words that passed between Chuck

Morgan and Betsy Mills. Now Clara leaned toward Johnny and asked in a low tone, 'What are you thinking about? I've been watching you. I thought I could hear the low hum of wheels spinning in your head.'

He winked at her. 'I guess you did. I was thinking it was hotter'n Hades in here and I was wondering if we could stand it until that outfit rides out of town.'

'Maybe Carl Sturtz will get here pretty soon with help,' she said. 'I guess we can stand it if he doesn't come, but it won't be easy. While ago I thought I was going to start screaming.'

'But you didn't.'

'No, I bit my tongue and held the screams back.' She nodded toward the Macks. 'But who knows? Maybe somebody else won't bite their tongue.'

'They'll have to scream and we'll have to listen,' he said. 'It's only a question till that bunch finds out we're in here.'

Clara's face was flushed, and when she moved the baby to a more comfortable position, Johnny saw that her dress where the child's face had been was wet. He turned to a bucket of water, poured some into a basin that was on the floor beside the bucket, and wet one end of a towel. He handed it to Clara who smiled her thanks and wiped and dried the baby's face.

'I've been thinking about my job,' Johnny said. 'I know we've talked about it a hundred

78

times, but we never get anything settled. I guess when you find yourself in a tight squeeze like this, you feel everything more sharply than you usually would.'

She nodded, her eyes questioning. 'I know how you feel, I've been thinking the same. Go on.'

'Well . . .' He swallowed, and then blurted, 'Damn it, maybe we can't change. Maybe we've just got to go on the way we are. I can't get a job on a ranch punching cows and make as much as I'm making. I just can't figure out any way to live cheaper than we're doing now.'

She nodded. 'I know about that, too. Don't forget. I buy the groceries. We skimp and scrape and we still get a little farther behind every month. Now our savings are gone.'

'Just $12.52 left in the savings account,' he said. 'We keep hoping every month that Jake Warner will give me a raise.'

'Old Skinflint Warner will give you a raise about as soon as that bunch of outlaws will turn into Santa Claus and his crew of helpers.' She shook her head, frowning. 'What makes me so darned mad is that Warner won't give you a nickel reward or even thank you for saving his money and risking your life doing it.'

'No, he sure won't,' Johnny agreed. 'The $12.52 will get us through one more month, then we'll have to borrow or not pay our store bill. What do you suppose Jake will say when I ask to borrow $50?'

'You know what he'll say,' Clara answered bitterly. 'He'll want to know what you've got for collateral and you'll say nothing and then he'll say no, let your wife and baby starve for all I care.'

That was just about the way it would go, Johnny told himself. He studied Clara's face. She was staring at Betsy and Chuck who were holding hands and whispering again. He wondered if Clara were wishing she wasn't married, if she had been honest when she had told Betsy she had not regretted for one little minute that she had married as young as she had.

There was a way out and he had mentioned it before, but Clara had always pushed the idea to one side. Now, because he felt completely frustrated and could not see any hope the way things stood, he tried again.

'Clara, your pa has a good farm down there by Wheatland,' he said. 'I can learn anything I don't know about farming. At least we . . .'

'No.' Her lips firmed out as she leaned forward. 'Listen to me, Johnny, and then don't ever bring it up again. My mother and I get along fine when we're fifty miles apart. When we're together we don't get along at all. I won't have her raising my children for me. We'll stay here and starve if we have to, but we will not move in with my folks.'

'All right,' he said. 'I won't mention it again.' He knew she felt that way, but he didn't know she felt so strongly about it. He had never been around her mother for more than a three or four day visit, so he didn't know her very well, but he guessed she would be like Elsie Mills if she and Clara were living in the same house. He couldn't think of anything worse than living with Elsie Mills.

Well, something would turn up. It had to. He would give himself one more month. If nothing else came along by that time, he'd try to get an evening job, maybe helping Carl Sturtz in the livery stable. Sturtz couldn't afford to pay more than a few dollars a month, but it would help.

Jake Warner would raise hell, saying it wasn't dignified for a banker to fork manure out of a livery stable, but Johnny had to do something. He'd tell Warner he'd have to raise his salary or let him work for Sturtz. It was that simple. If Warner fired him, well, maybe he'd be better off. Sometimes bad luck turned out to be good luck in disguise.

He glanced at the flour sack that held the bank's money. It would be very easy to take a few dollars out of the sack sometime during the day. He could have done it when he dropped the money into the sack. He could still do it when this trouble was over and he returned the money to the safe.

Sure, Jake Warner would count it and he'd know some was missing, but Johnny could say it had been lost out of the sack or it had been stolen during the day by one of the other persons in the jail. Warner could never prove Johnny took it.

Just fifty or sixty dollars would help so much. He could tell himself over and over that he had it coming, that he had actually earned that money. Then he rose and turned to the loophole near the door, knowing this was wasted thinking. He could never do it.

A man yelled from the front of the saloon, 'You hear me, you people in the jail?'

Chuck Morgan jumped up and peered through a loophole. Baldy Mack who had seemed lost in his thoughts or perhaps had dropped off to sleep now got up, and looked out through the nearest window.

'Don't answer,' Johnny ordered. 'Not any of you.'

The man who was yelling was the outlaw leader, Black Jack Connor. He went on shouting, saying he wanted the dinero that had been in the bank and Smith would be a dead man if they didn't bring the money to him in an hour, then he went back into the saloon.

'Give it to 'em,' Baldy Mack said. 'Let's get out of this hell hole. He said they'd ride out of town and not hurt any of us.'

Mrs. Mack nodded. 'It's the best chance we've got. I want to save the store.'

Chuck and Betsy were looking at him, too, nodding and agreeing with the Macks. Johnny didn't look at Clara. He knew she was worried about the baby and he was afraid to find out what she thought.

'No,' Johnny said. 'We won't give the money to them.'

'Why not?' Mack demanded.

Mrs. Mack walked toward Johnny. 'Yes, why not? You owe Jake Warner absolutely nothing the way he's treated you. They can keep us penned up here all day if Carl Sturtz don't bring any help. All night, too. We'll go crazy. Let 'em take the money and leave town. It's all we can ask for.'

'That's the point,' Johnny said. 'They won't. You can't believe anything Connor promises. He'll kill us as soon as he gets the money and he'll burn the town. The only chance we've got to stay alive is to keep the money and not show up in the street.'

'How do you know that?' Betsy asked.

'By the way they killed Chuck's grandpa,' Johnny answered, 'and from what Carl Sturtz said about them.'

'Hogwash,' Mack said. 'Sturtz was scared. You can't believe what he said. I think Connor will keep his word.'

Funny, Johnny thought as he looked at Baldy Mack. The storekeeper had been scared into a sort of trance, scared so much he had even tried to run away. Now he was talking big just as he had when they'd first made their plans early that morning and he expected everyone to listen to him.

Johnny walked to the door and put his hands on the bar. 'I'll open the door, Baldy, and you and Mrs. Mack run outside. Be quick about it because I don't want to leave the door open very long.'

'Keep it shut,' Mrs. Mack said wearily. 'We'll stay.'

'You don't have to,' Johnny said. 'Go on over to your store and tell that wolf pack you wanted to give them the money, but I wouldn't let you.'

'Go to hell,' Mack said and sat down again, his back to the wall, his head between his knees.

Mrs Mack laughed shortly. 'Maybe you're right, Johnny. They're a bad lot and maybe we shouldn't trust them. I just hate to see Limpy Smith murdered.'

'We tried to get him to stay with us,' Johnny said. 'It was his idea to go back to the saloon, not ours. He could have been safe if he'd stayed here.'

Mrs. Mack turned away, not answering. It was noon now and some of the outlaws had apparently slipped out through the alley door because Johnny, watching through a window, saw them dart around the corner at the end of the block and go into the café.

They were playing it safe, and Johnny wondered why Connor had stood up over there in front of the saloon when he'd yelled his ultimatum. He'd made a sizable target, but

84

maybe as leader of a gang like this he could not afford to act as if he were afraid of anything.

Judging from the short shadows that fell into the dust of the street it was noon or later. Nobody had said anything about being hungry. Johnny guessed that no one in the jail wanted to eat, not even the baby.

CHAPTER TWELVE

Black Jack Connor had no intention of killing Limpy Smith, not because he liked the saloon man or pitied him or even believed what he had said about staying out of the jail so he could wait on them. It was a simple proposition that Smith could be useful as long as he was alive. He just didn't foresee that Cutter Doon's hoorawing would get out of hand.

Cutter Doon lacked the guts to take his anger out on Black Jack. The anger was there, all right, locked up inside him. He had done most of the work putting this gang together and it was understood that he was second in command, but in reality he amounted to nothing.

It was Black Jack all the way. Apparently it never occurred to him to ask Doon's advice or to delegate authority to him. His practical joke of setting fire to the bunk and throwing water on Doon while he was sleeping that morning had been the last straw.

Needing a scapegoat, Cutter Doon turned to Limpy Smith. He sensed the rabbit quality of the man, so he said loudly to Black Jack, 'It struck me that our bartender was a good man to stay out of jail and come over here to wait for us. Looks to me like we owe him something.'

'Good?' Black Jack laughed his humorless laugh. 'Hell, the only thing that's good to him is a hunk of dinero he can hold in his hand. That right, Smith?'

'I was thinking you'd be paying for the drinks your boys are having,' Smith said. 'I'm doing my part, tending bar for you and furnishing the whisky.'

'You see?' Doon slapped his leg and laughed. 'He's doing his part. Let's take his pants off. I'd like to see him serving drinks with his shirttail flapping.'

The men laughed, but Smith saw no humor in what Doon had said. He faced his tormenter, the corners of his mouth working. 'You let me alone. You're as bad as Carl Sturtz said you were. You don't have to pay me nothing. Just let me alone.'

'You're right about one thing,' Doon said. 'We don't have to pay you for nothing.'

'Carl Sturtz,' Black Jack said thoughtfully, staring at Smith. 'That name sure sounds familiar. Who is he?'

'He owns the livery stable,' Smith answered.

'Sure,' Cutter Doon said. 'You remember this morning the old man said maybe we could swap horses with him . . .'

Irritated, Black Jack broke in, 'Yeah, I remember, but I hadn't heard his first name was Carl. That's what makes it sound familiar.'

'He used to be a law man,' Smith said. 'U.S. Marshal, I think he was. He's a deputy now. He rode out for Douglas early this morning to get help.'

When Billy Horn heard it, he got up from the table and crossed the room to Black Jack. He said harshly, 'You hear that? We'll have a posse on our tails in another hour or two. Are we gonna fight 'em, or get our hands on that dinero and bust the breeze riding out of here?'

'We'll get the dinero,' Black Jack snapped. Suddenly he pounded the bar with the palm of his hand. 'Now I remember. I knew him when I was a kid. He was a town marshal. I disremember where it was. Some cow town in Kansas. Dodge City probably. Hell, he's an old man now and probably all bunged up with rheumatism. I don't reckon he'll ever get here with a posse.'

Nobody was paying any attention to him. The other men in the room were staring at Cutter Doon who had pulled a knife out of his pocket and opened a blade. Now he ran a finger along the edge as he said, 'My pappy

87

gave me this knife before he died. We had a farm in Arizona and he always used it to cut his hogs. It ain't been used for a long time, but I reckon it'll still do the job.' He winked at Billy Horn. 'What do you think, Billy?'

'If it was sharp enough to cut hogs,' Horn answered, 'it'll cut a bartender.'

'That's what I was thinking,' Doon said, 'but I wasn't sure. Let's find out.'

He started toward Limpy Smith, the knife held in front of him. For a moment the saloon man held his ground, staring at Doon as if thinking the outlaw didn't mean it, then he let out a yelp of agonizing fear and wheeled and lunged for the door.

'Don't let him get away,' Black Jack bellowed.

There was nobody close enough to the back door to stop him. Smith would have escaped if he had reached the door, but he never made it. Cutter Doon drew his gun and shot Smith in the back between the shoulder blades. He staggered two steps, then his knees gave way and he sprawled on the floor.

For a moment Black Jack stared at the dead man, then a wave of black fury swept over him, not because Limpy Smith was dead, but because Cutter Doon had done the killing without asking his permission.

'You fool!' Black Jack said, 'You brainless idiot! You had no call to beef him.'

Cutter Doon and Horn dragged the body

through the face filled with resentment. 'You're a good one to be saying that,' he said. 'You've been killing men without no call for doing it ever since we started out.'

'That's right,' Billy Horn said. 'It's what I've been saying all along. Your killing ain't got us nothing except to put more men on our tail.'

Black Jack's right hand eased toward his gun, then dropped away as cold reason worked through the fury. Doon had his gun in his hand and Billy Horn was standing with his hand splayed over the butt of his gun. His knees were slightly bent; he was like a tightly coiled steel spring ready to be released. He would be fast, Black Jack told himself. What he had intended to do would be suicide.

'All right,' he said with feigned carelessness as he turned toward the bar. 'Small loss. Drag him outside, Cutter. I never like to look at a man's carcass.'

Cutter Doon and Horn dragged the body through the back door. They left it in the alley and came back. Black Jack poured himself a drink and stood motionless, staring at the amber liquid for a time, then began to slowly turn the glass with the tips of his fingers.

His hatred for people grew and took complete possession of him, not just the good people who obeyed the laws and deposited money in the banks and paid their taxes. He hated everyone including Cutter Doon who was his only friend in the outfit.

That is, Cutter Doon had been his friend, Black Jack told himself, but maybe he wasn't now. Black Jack wasn't sure why Doon had killed Smith, but an idea began festering in his mind. Doon might have done it to provoke a quarrel; maybe he had gone over to Billy Horn who had been trying to force a showdown fight for some time.

He heard one of the men say, 'Ain't it dinner time? All I know is I ain't et since breakfast and that was mighty early this morning.'

And another, 'Yeah, it sure was. My tapeworm's been growling for an hour and now it's started to bark.'

Black Jack turned to face them. He said, 'Billy, you and Slim and Ugly Pete and Big Nose go over to the café. I guess you can talk this Mills woman into feeding you.'

Billy Horn nodded. 'We'll talk her into it, all right.'

He started toward the batwings. 'Hold on,' Black Jack said. 'Go out through the back door and down the alley to the end of the block. Chances are you can get to the café without being seen from the jail. For not more'n a few seconds, anyhow, if you get a move on. When you're in the café, go out behind it and take a look at the back wall of the jail. See if there are any windows or a door on that side.'

Horn scratched his stubble-covered cheek.

'I reckon you want us to stay out of the street on account of that bunch in the jail might start shooting one of these times, but what difference does it make it there's windows or a door in the back?'

'We've got to open that jail up someway,' Black said wearily as if Horn were an idiot not to know the answer to his question. 'When we rode into town, I seen the west wall and it ain't got any windows. Same with the east wall you can see from the front of the saloon. Now if the back ain't got windows or a door, I figure somebody could go from the store to the back of the jail and blow the wall out with a charge of dynamite. Cutter's an expert with dynamite and chances are we'll find plenty in the store to do the job.'

Horn nodded. 'That'll work,' he said. 'We ought to be getting at it. That posse may show up any time.'

Black Jack shook his head. 'I don't figure we'll see that posse till evening and probably not then. Carl Sturtz is an old man like I told you. The sheriff in Douglas don't figure to stir his stumps for an old booger like Sturtz.'

He motioned toward the back door. 'Get moving. The rest of us will be along after while, so tell her to keep the stove hot. I don't want everybody over there at one time. Might scare her so bad she couldn't cook good.'

The four men disappeared through the alley door. Black Jack picked up his glass, downed the drink, and set the glass back on the polished cherrywood. Cutter Doon moved to the bar and stood beside him.

'You never asked me if I'd use the dynamite,' he said.

'I never ask a man when I'm ramrodding an outfit like this,' Black Jack said. 'I tell him, but there is something I'll ask you. Why did you smoke Smith down while ago?'

'You said to stop him,' Doon answered sullenly, 'so I did. There wasn't nobody between him and the door. I figured you didn't want him throwing in with the bunch that's holed up in the jail.'

'I guess it wouldn't have made much difference either way,' Black Jack said. 'We'll get the dinero purty soon. It just looked to me like you was trying to kick up some dust. You had no call to hooraw Smith in the first place.'

'Why should I kick up any dust?' Doon demanded. 'Maybe you don't know, but Billy Horn's the one. He's been kicking up a storm. It won't take much for the rest of the outfit to throw in with Billy and leave you talking to yourself.'

'I know,' Black Jack said wearily. 'Maybe we've all got to the end of the line. When an outfit starts cracking up inside, it ain't gonna last much longer.' He turned his head and pinned his gaze on Doon's face. 'But I figured I could count on you.'

Doon met Black Jack's gaze for a moment,

then turned his eyes away. 'Sure, you can count on me. I'll take care of the dynamiting.'

'Good,' Black Jack said as he turned away and walked to the batwings and pushed through them to stand on the boardwalk.

'Don't get no notion about smoking me down,' he yelled. 'Several of my boys are in the café. Mrs. Mills gets a slug through her head the minute you open up on me. Your hour's gone. Limpy Smith's dead. If you don't turn that dinero over to us in a hurry, Mrs. Mills will be dead, too. In that case, we will burn the town. If you've got any sense, you'll see we get the money pronto and save yourself a lot of trouble.'

He wheeled and went back into the saloon. He wiped his face, grinning a little. He had expected them to shoot at him, but no one had the guts to start it. Now they would go on with the cat and mouse game. It was fun, he told himself, about as much fun as he would have before he cashed in. It didn't make much difference now. All he wanted was to take a few with him when he went.

He nodded at the other four men who were waiting for dinner, 'Go on over to the café and eat. The ones that are there ought to be about done. Me'n Cutter will be along purty soon,'

They left. Cutter Doon still stood by the bar staring at Black Jack. He said, 'I guess the notion that I might be hungry never entered your head.'

'I've got better plans for us,' Black Jack said, 'so I figured we could wait. We don't want the rest of the bunch around when we're with this Elsie Mills.'

'Well now,' Doon said, pleased with the prospect, 'I hadn't thought of that.'

Black Jack went to the bar and poured himself another drink. There wasn't much time left, but what the hell! One more drink, one more square meal, one more woman to bed down with. That was all there was to life. In a little while it would be gone.

He wasn't going to make it to the Colorado mountains and get that last drink of sweet, cold water. He didn't know how he knew but he did know. He was sure of it. Just about himself. He didn't know about the others, but before he cashed in, he'd finish that stubborn bunch that was hanging onto the money. He didn't know why those people were so stubborn. They'd have no use for it in hell.

Funny thing, he told himself, that he had come to the end of the trail in this stinking, little burg that had to hire an old, broken-down, has-been of a lawman for a deputy. He looked across the bar at his reflection in the mirror. Nothing left for him, he thought. If he didn't get a dose of hot lead in Platte City, he'd get it somewhere else. Any way he looked at it, dying of lead poisoning was better than dancing on nothing with a rope around his neck.

CHAPTER THIRTEEN

The people in the jail heard the shot that killed Limpy Smith. For a long time they remained silent, not wanting to look at each other. All of them felt the burden of guilt. The one who felt it the least was Johnny Roan because he felt Smith had brought it on himself.

Mrs. Mack brought her gaze to Johnny's face and opened her mouth, but before she could get a word out, he said, 'Don't say it. I'm not to blame for Limpy Smith's murder. Neither are you. Remember what I said while ago. He made the decision. We didn't. He thought he'd make a few dollars from selling whisky to the outlaws. Now he's dead.'

'But we could have saved him,' Mrs. Mack cried. 'They warned us. If we had given them the money . . .'

'Let's not keep going over it,' Johnny said roughly. 'I'm damned tired of arguing. When a man or woman is stubborn enough to risk their lives, it's their business, not ours. We can't decide everything for them.'

'That's right,' Clara agreed. 'I think the only person in this room with any sense is Johnny. We made our decision early this morning when Chuck brought word of his grandfather's murder. All of us made that decision.' She looked directly at Mrs. Mack. 'Now let's stick to it.'

Chuck ran the tip of his tongue over dry lips. 'That's all we can do,' he said. 'I seen 'em kill grandpa, so I know what that bunch will do. I'm glad to be alive. I want to stay alive and I want Betsy alive.'

Betsy looked at Chuck and then at Johnny. 'Why don't we say it right out loud? We're all thinking the same thing. Mamma's going to be next.'

'She made the same decision Limpy did,' Clara reminded her. 'You can't blame Johnny or any of the rest of us for what your mother decided. I've worked for her, Betsy. I know her better than anyone here except you. Maybe I know her better than you do. She never took anybody's advice in her life and she sure didn't change this morning.'

They all knew it was true, yet now that they faced what was certain to happen, they turned away from it because they could not erase the sense of guilt, all except Johnny who said, 'Nothing's changed.'

Then he closed his eyes as he leaned against the wall and wiped the sweat from his forehead with his sleeve. He felt guilty, too, not because he thought they could have done or said anything that morning which would have changed Elsie Mills's mind, but because he hoped they would kill her. He had a very definite feeling that everybody in Platte City would be happier if Elsie were dead, especially Betsy and Chuck.

If Elsie Mills lived to be one hundred years old, she would never be a decent human being. She grew worse with the years instead of better. There just wasn't any hope for her. Then he wished he hadn't thought what he had. Having thought it, he felt guiltier than ever.

Probably Betsy wanted her mother dead, too. Elsie Mills had made the girl's life miserable for her from the day she was born, but Betsy could not admit it to herself or anyone else. Johnny, of course, could not say to her, 'Betsy, let's just hold off doing anything about your mother and let them murder her. You'll be happier when she's dead. You could marry Chuck if she was out of the way.'

Johnny got up and walked to the back of the jail, stirring the dust as he walked. Oh no, you can't say or even think what is honest. He had never known a bitchier woman than Elsie Mills, or a more bullheaded one. To him the fact that she had brought this on herself was the important factor. He told himself again that whatever happened, he was not going to risk the lives of the people who were here with him or give up the bank's money for Elsie Mills.

It came, then, just as they had known it would. Black Jack Connor was yelling at them again, saying if they didn't get the money in a few minutes, Mrs. Mills would be dead and the town would burn.

As soon as he disappeared into the saloon, Mrs. Mack screamed at Johnny, 'You see? It's just like I told you while ago. If we give them the money, we'll save Elsie's life and the town, too.'

'And your store,' Johnny added.

'Yes, our store,' Mrs. Mack flung at him. 'Is there anything wrong with that?'

'No, there's nothing wrong with that,' Johnny said, 'but why didn't you and Baldy stay in the store this morning? You could have sold them grub and guns and shells and made a lot of money.'

'The way Limpy did,' Clara added. 'I know how you feel, but I want to live and I don't want to be raped by those men and I don't want Johnny killed.'

'Better think about it,' Johnny said. 'By the time you and Clara and Betsy are raped as often as those ten men can do it, you'll be dead. If you're not, you'll kill yourself.'

Betsy was sitting beside Chuck beneath a window. Now she got up and came to Johnny. 'But she is my mother. I know how she is. If she'd had her way, I'd be in the café with her, but I'll never forgive myself if they kill her and all the time there was something I could do and I didn't do it.'

'There's nothing, Betsy,' Johnny said. 'Nothing. You make your decision and you live

98

or die by it. Elsie made her decision this morning to die. So did Limpy. We decided to sweat it out in here and live. That's the way it's going to be.'

Baldy was standing beside the wall, the rifle in his hands. Beads of sweat stood out all over his face and ran down his nose and on to the point of his chin, then dripped onto his shirt. He said in a quivery voice, 'You've got the only ticket there is to get 'em out of town and keep it from burning and save our lives and the store. Give 'em the money. It ain't yours. It won't hurt you none to lose it.'

'That's right,' Johnny said. 'It's not mine. That's the reason I can't give it away.'

Mrs. Mack shook her head. 'That's the part I don't understand, Johnny. It's Jake Warner's money. Jake's treated you like a dirty shirt from the day you went to work for him, but now you're bound to get the town burned just to keep Jake's money for him.'

'It's not Jake's money,' Johnny said, his temper threatening to get away from him. She was a businesswoman and she knew better. 'It's the bank's money. It belongs to all of us in this room and everybody in town and the ranchers all around here. If I give the money up, the bank closes its doors and the country is ruined. Can't you see that?'

'It's Elsie's life I'm trying to save,' Mrs. Mills said stubbornly. 'A woman. It's not like it was a while ago when we were talking about Limpy.

What's money when you can save a woman's life with it?'

'If I was able to get out of here and if I went to the café,' Johnny said, 'do you think for a minute I could talk Mrs. Mills into coming back with me as long as she's got a chance to sell a hot dinner to the outlaws?'

'Give them the money and they'll leave town,' Mrs. Mack said.

Betsy dabbed at her eyes and nodded. 'I don't want you to get killed, Johnny, but it's my mother's life we're talking about. If the outlaws were gone, she couldn't sell them a hot dinner.'

Johnny looked from one to the other on to Baldy Mack who hadn't moved for several minutes. He felt completely frustrated. They weren't reasoning now, none except Clara who was still on his side. He doubted that Chuck knew how he felt, but there was no doubt about how the other three felt.

They hated him, he thought bitterly, or they would after Elsie Mills was killed and the store burned. He wondered if the day would come when he would hate himself for not giving up and handing the money over to Black Jack Connor. He heard the baby whimper and watched Clara pick him up and hold him. He knew then he would not hate himself, not unless he lost his guts and caved in.

Johnny looked more closely at Baldy Mack. There was something wrong with his eyes.

Johnny wondered if the man was out of his mind. The thought occurred to him that Baldy might be going crazy under the pressure of danger and would use his rifle on the people inside the jail, starting with him.

Mrs. Mack stood in the center of the room thirty feet from her husband. She kept staring at Johnny as if determined to find a way to force him to change his mind. Now Johnny went to her and whispered, 'If Baldy goes loco and looks like he's going to shoot his way out of here, I'll kill him. You'd better run mighty close herd on him.'

Mrs. Mack hesitated, then she said, 'I'll watch him,' and turned toward her husband.

Johnny walked to a window and stared through a dusty pane into the street. He had said all he could; he had done all he could which was exactly nothing. There was no more to be done except wait for the next event in a tragedy that was destined as surely as the sunset.

CHAPTER FOURTEEN

Black Jack waited in the saloon until Billy Horn returned with the three men who had gone to the café with him. Horn was digging at his teeth with a toothpick. All four had the satisfied expression of men who had just filled their bellies.

Horn helped himself to a cigar from the box on the bar. He bit off an end, put the cigar into his mouth and lighted it, then pulled on it and blew out a cloud of smoke. He said, 'I'll say one thing for that old heifer even if she is shaped like a tub of lard and she's got a face that would scare a bull into the next county. She can cook a steak.'

'You get a look at the back of the jail?' Black Jack demanded.

Horn nodded. 'Nothing there. Just a wall. Maybe some loopholes. I couldn't see for sure from where I was, but there ain't no windows and no door.'

'Good,' Black Jack said. 'Come on, Cutter, let's put the feed bag on. After we eat we'll go to the store and look for dynamite. Billy, keep an eye on the jail till I get back.'

Horn chewed on his cigar, apparently puzzled by Black Jack's request. He had seldom been asked by Black Jack to do anything more important than to saddle up or feed and water the horses. He shrugged and said, 'Sure, I'll watch 'em,' and tongued the cigar to the other side of his mouth.

When Black Jack and Cutter Doon were in the alley, Doon said, 'When we get this caper wound up, you're going to have to have it out with Billy.'

'It'll be a pleasure,' Black Jack said.

They reached the side street, rounded the

last building in the block, and quickly crossed the street to the café. When they went in, they found the second group of men sitting at the counter finishing their pie. Black Jack started to say something, but before he got a word out, Elsie Mills came out of the kitchen with a steaming coffee pot.

Black Jack whispered, 'My God!' He stared at her until she filled the four cups on the counter; then he said, 'Two more steaks.'

She looked at him, scowling, sweat dribbling down her face. 'You the big chief of this outfit?'

'I'm it,' Black Jack said.

'I've served eight dinners and you're asking for two more,' she said. 'I'm telling you right now I ain't working for nothing. So far nobody's paid. How about it? You paying for all of 'em?'

'You'll get what's coming to you,' Black Jack said curtly. 'Now get a move on.'

'Nobody talks to me that way and nobody hurries me,' Elsie Mills said. 'I don't care if you are the high cock-a-roarum of this gang and if you're ten feet tall. You ain't . . .'

'All right, all right,' Black Jack said testily. 'Just get our dinners.'

She stood staring at him for several seconds, still scowling, then turned and stalked back into the kitchen. 'I wouldn't have believed it if I hadn't seen it,' Black Jack said. He nodded at the first man at the counter. 'How was your steak, Miggs?'

'Damned good,' the man said. 'So's the pie and coffee.'

Black Jack motioned for Cutter Doon to sit down at the counter, then took the stool next to him. 'I hope they're right about her cooking,' he said. 'Horn sure didn't make no mistake about her face and shape.'

'Sure you want her?' Doon asked.

Black Jack shrugged. 'Looks like she's all there is. A man can always shut his eyes.' He cuffed his hat back to the back of his head with his thumb, then added, 'Miggs, as soon as you finish that coffee, go into the store through the back door and look for dynamite. Don't do nothing with it. Wait for Cutter. Soon as we get done here, he'll be over and help you fix it so you'll blow the whole back end of the jail loose.'

'Suits me,' Miggs said as he slid off the stool. 'This damned town is a furnace. The sooner we get the dinero and start riding, the better I'll like it.'

After the four men finished eating and left the café, Elsie Mills brought two plates almost covered by the steaks. She returned with fried potatoes and biscuits, then filled their coffee cups. The men ate, Black Jack admitting to himself with the first bite that Horn and Miggs had been right. He had never tasted a better steak in his life. A few minutes later she set their pieces of pie in front of them with a banging clatter that jarred Black Jack's nerves.

'You're a noisy old heifer,' he said. 'Do you have to make so much racket?'

She glared at him from the other side of the counter, her hands on her hips. 'You have got no room to talk, mister. You eat like a hog. I never heard so much chomping in my life.'

Black Jack had just filled his mouth with a bit of steak. Now he almost choked on it as he tipped his head back and glared at her. He heard Cutter Doon snicker and was tempted to knock the man off his stool. He had never had a woman talk to him that way. She was a fool or drunk, or maybe the toughest female he had ever run into. He was inclined to think it was the latter.

'She's got a mean tongue, now ain't she?' Cutter Doon said. 'Maybe we oughtta cut it out of her head.'

'I want my money,' Mrs. Mills said. 'I've been working in that hell-hot kitchen all morning fixing grub for you and your boys and I aim to get paid for it.'

Cutter Doon pulled his knife out of his pocket, opened it, and ran the forefinger of his right hand along the edge of the blade. 'Pull her tongue out, Jack. I'll bet it's a foot long. Pull it out and I'll whack it off.'

'You'll whack nothing,' the woman said. 'Just gimme my money and finish your pie and get to hell out of my place.'

'Put that knife away.' Black Jack looked at

Elsie Mills again. 'You know who I am?'

She shrugged her shoulders. 'They say you're Black Jack Connor, which same makes me no never mind. The only thing that counts with me is the money I've got coming.'

'Ever hear of me before?'

'Not till that old goat of a Carl Sturtz started talking,' she answered.

'And just what did that old goat say about me?' Black Jack asked softly.

'Nothing that was good,' she said. 'You wouldn't want to hear it.'

'Sure I do.'

'Well, he had some wild tale about you getting out of Yuma and being a real salty son of a bitch,' she said. 'I didn't take no stock in it. I figured you'd be hungry the same as any man and you'd eat my cooking which you done and then pay me for it which you ain't done.' She laughed harshly. 'Don't get the idea you're walking out of here without paying. I've handled tougher men than you and don't you forget it.'

'I'd never auger with you about that.' He finished his pie and coffee and rose. Elsie Mills still stood behind the counter, glaring at him as she waited for her money. Black Jack stretched and grinned as he asked, 'Where's your bedroom?'

'Bedroom?' For the first time Mrs. Mills was visibly shaken as she took a step backward toward the kitchen, her face turning pale.

'What do you want to know about my bedroom for?'

'That's where we're going,' he said. 'Come on, Cutter. Let's get this over with so we can finish our business and get out of this stinking town.'

Elsie Mills stared at him as if she still couldn't believe what they intended to do, then she blurted, 'Sturtz was right. I didn't think that old fool could be right about anything. I thought he was all blow.'

'Right about what?'

'He said you were crazy enough to rape any woman you could find and kill all the men you could just for the fun of it and maybe burn the town.' She shook her head as if she still did not believe it. 'You might be crazy enough to kill some men for fun and burn the town, but I don't believe you could be crazy enough to rape me.'

'That's being purty crazy, all right,' Black Jack said, 'but we owe you a little pleasure after you went to all the trouble to cook for us. We don't have no money to give you, so this is the best we can do for you.'

Cutter Doon snickered again. 'I get the notion she don't think it's gonna be much pleasure.'

She had backed along the counter until she stood in the kitchen doorway. She said, 'I know damned well it wouldn't be, not by a man as ugly as you.'

Black Jack laughed. 'She's got an eye for beauty, and she don't see none on your ugly mug.'

'Maybe I ain't no beauty,' Cutter Doon said sullenly, 'but by God, I don't see how she can talk. I never seen an uglier woman than she is.'

'You ain't no purtier'n he is,' she said, nodding at Black Jack. 'Why sons of bitches like you think you're God's gift to women is more'n I know. Now git out of here. You ain't man enough to do it, neither one of you.'

'May take both of us,' Black Jack said. 'Come on, Cutter. The bedroom must be back here.'

He started toward her, but she had backed up as far as she was going to. She waited until he was a step away, then she hit him in the stomach with her fist. He doubled over, his breath driven out of him. Shocked, Cutter Doon said, 'You shouldn't of done that, Mrs. Mills. We wasn't aiming to hurt you, but you're going to get hurt now.'

'So you weren't aiming to hurt me,' she mimicked: 'You was sure putting on a job of play acting.'

She turned toward a kitchen shelf and started reaching for something. Doon drew his gun. 'Stand pat,' he ordered. 'I suppose you've got a gun hidden back there somewhere. You lay a hand on it and I'll kill you. I don't like killing women, but I can do it.'

Black Jack had regained his wind. He

straightened up as Elsie Mills dropped her hand to her side, her gaze whipping from one to the other. Now, for the first time she seemed to sense the total depravity of these men and began to tremble. 'Don't,' she begged. 'Don't do it.'

She started to run toward her bedroom, but she was too slow. Black Jack grabbed her by a shoulder and yanked her around to face him. Then he hit her just as he would have hit a man, his fist rocking her head. He grabbed the front of her dress and ripped it away from her body.

She was hurt, but not hurt enough to give up. She grabbed a frying pan off the stove and swung it. Black Jack yelled something at her, and tried to dodge, but he was too late.

If the blow had caught him squarely on the head, it might have killed him. As it was, he went down to the floor on his face, the crack of the heavy pan on his head the same sound a pole ax makes on the skull of a beef.

Cutter Doon acted from sheer instinct. He had his gun in his hand, he had a terrifying feeling that Black Jack had been brained. He fired twice: he saw the woman driven back by the impact of the bullets until she fell against her work table. Her big body rolled off to the floor and lay still.

CHAPTER FIFTEEN

The people in the jail did not say anything when they heard the two shots from the café. They had been expecting them; they knew what the shots meant. In a way it was a relief to hear them. For the moment at least the tension was eased.

Johnny Roan did not understand this. He had supposed Mrs. Mack would start blaming him for Elsie Mills' murder; he expected her and some of the others, too, to start insisting once more that he turn the money over to the outlaws in exchange for a promise to get out of town. But no one said a word for several minutes.

Baldy Mack sat with his back to the wall, his rifle across his lap. He didn't move a muscle. He might have been in some kind of trance, but he'd been in and out of something like that almost from the time the outlaws had come to town.

Johnny wasn't sure yet whether the man was pretending or not. His wife sat beside him. She was as motionless as he was, the only sign of life the pounding of blood in her temples.

Betsy Mills held back her tears as long as she could, then the dam broke. She suddenly let out a shrill cry that was almost a scream, and buried her face in the front of Chuck's shirt, She began to sob, great, body-shaking, strangling sobs with a long pause between that made Johnny wonder if she was going to catch her next breath.

Chuck held her in his arms and patted her on the back as he muttered, 'The sons of bitches. The dirty sons of bitches.'

Johnny wiped his face with his handkerchief. It didn't do much good. The sweat broke out through his pores immediately. He looked at Clara who was sitting beside her baby. He thought she should go to Betsy and say something, but Clara seemed to have the notion the girl would have no peace until she cried herself into a state of exhaustion.

Finally he could stand it no longer and went to Betsy and knelt beside her. He said, 'I'm sorry. It was my fault. I should have tried to make a deal with Connor.'

He was surprised to hear himself saying that. He guessed it made him a first class idiot. He had resented being blamed for Smith's and Elsie Mills' death, yet now he was blaming himself.

Chuck shook his head at Johnny. He said, 'No, you ain't to blame.'

Betsy sat back and wiped her eyes and stopped crying. For a time her lips trembled and she was unable to say anything. Then she whispered, 'Nobody's blaming you, Johnny. Nobody's to blame but Ma herself. She always was too bullheaded to listen to anyone else.'

'We know one thing for sure,' Clara said. 'We know just how awful and bloodthirsty these men are. We know what will happen to us if they get in here or they get us outside.'

Mrs. Mack nodded and said nothing. Baldy had come out of the fog again for a moment. He raised his head and asked, 'Where's Carl Sturtz and the posse he was fetching to get us out of here?'

Johnny had been afraid somebody would ask that. All he knew was that Sturtz had been gone long enough to bring a posse. The fact that it hadn't come was a pretty good indication it wasn't coming, that Sturtz had failed to get any cooperation from the sheriff in Douglas. That meant, then, that it was a question of who would break first, the outlaws who were outside and free and who wanted the bank money, or the people who were penned up inside the jail and were safe as long as they stayed there.

The outlaws probably were being pursued. If so, they would want to get moving again. Johnny didn't know much about things like this, and he had no way of measuring their thoughts and feelings, but it seemed to him that the outlaws must have a breaking point, trapped between their greed and their fear of being caught by a pursuing posse.

The baby started to cry. Clara picked him up and began talking to him. She paced back and forth, stirring the dust as she walked. Johnny stood watching, feeling helpless as he always did when the baby cried for what seemed no reason.

'He's so hot,' Clara said. 'His face is awfully red. He must have a fever.'

Johnny dipped the towel into the water again and wrung it out and handed it to Clara. She wiped the baby's face, but the water was too warm to have much cooling effect.

Clara gave the towel back. She said in a low voice, 'I've got to get him outside. It's stifling in here. He can't breathe.'

'You can't go out,' Johnny said.

She knew she couldn't and he wondered why she said it. She looked at him and ran the tip of her tongue over her cracked lips. She said, 'Johnny, these men are animals, but even animals are fond of babies. They wouldn't hurt me if they knew the baby was sick and I had to . . .'

'Of course they would,' he said. 'They're worse than animals. All they'd know is that you're a woman.'

She shook her head. 'I don't believe it. I'm going to try it.'

He grabbed her shoulders more roughly than he intended. 'No you're not,' he said in a low, tight voice. 'Now you listen to me. The baby won't die of any fever he's got from it being so hot in here. Haven't I got enough trouble from the others without you adding to it?'

She started to say something, then tears ran down her cheeks and she turned away, saying, 'I'm sorry, Johnny.'

He walked around the wall, examining it carefully and trying to put Clara and the baby out of his mind. He had looked at this building day after day for years, but he couldn't remember for sure whether there used to be another door besides the big one next to the street.

If he could find another way out of the building, he'd allow Clara and the baby to leave for a little while, long enough to get some fresh air anyhow. As long as the outlaws remained in the saloon or the café, they wouldn't see Clara if there was another opening in the side or rear walls.

Now that he thought about it, he seemed to remember that a long time ago there had been another door in the rear wall. It had been filled with stone to look like the rest of the wall, although he could not remember the reason it had been done. If that was true, there was a possibility the job had been a hasty one and the stones could be removed.

He heard Baldy Mack's voice again, 'How about Carl Sturtz and the posse? Ain't Carl coming to get us out of here?'

'They'll be along after while,' Mrs. Mack said patiently. 'We'll just have to wait for them.'

At least she had stopped demanding that he make a deal with Connor, Johnny thought. Glancing at them, he saw that Mrs. Mack hadn't moved and Baldy had lapsed back into that strange, trance-like condition, his head tipped forward, his chin against his chest. The baby was still crying. Clara put him back on the blanket and gave him a drink of water, but it didn't help.

Chuck sat against the wall where he had been, his arm around Betsy who had her head on his shoulder. They just made each other hotter, Johnny thought sourly. Why didn't they know enough to separate?

He went on, feeling along the wall and wondering if he had just dreamed there had once been a second door that had been filled with cement and stone. Then he found it on the back wall and saw immediately that he had wasted his time.

The door had been filled with stone and the mortar was as hard as any of the rest of the wall. He might just as well attempt to dig his way out through any other part of the building as to try to remove these stones. He guessed he had known all the time that it would be this way. It was just that he had to have something to do.

Suddenly Baldy Mack yelled, 'Can't you stop that kid's infernal bawling?'

'No,' Clara said. ' I would if I could.'

Mrs. Mack shot a glance at Johnny who

walked toward them, his fists clenched. She said to her husband, 'Shhh.' Then she rose and met Johnny before he reached Baldy. She whispered, 'Try to overlook that. I don't know what to do any more than you do. I won't argue with you any more about letting them have the money. Not since Elsie was murdered and I don't doubt that she has been. Before that I kept thinking these men were human beings and we could deal with them. I don't think so after I heard the shots. I don't want to leave here or even open the door and give them a chance to get in.'

Johnny looked past her at Baldy who had tipped his head forward again. He had a strong suspicion the man was feigning this condition. He wouldn't have to do any fighting if it came to that.

'What about Baldy?' he asked. 'He was all right this morning. I always took him for a pretty good man, but he's either acting, which makes him a first class coward, or he's out of his head.'

'He's not acting,' she said. 'I should have known this might happen. He did it once before when the pressure was so great he couldn't stand it. I'd forgotten because it was a long time ago and I thought it would never happen again.' Johnny didn't believe her. Whatever was done would have to be done by him and an eighteen-year-old boy who had never been forced to stand up and fight in a situation like this. Hell, Johnny thought, he wasn't much better, but he guessed it didn't make any difference about age or what you had done in the past. Everything depended on what a man could do today.

When Johnny didn't say anything more about Baldy, Mrs. Mack asked, 'You don't think Carl's coming with the posse, do you?'

'Doesn't look like it,' Johnny admitted.

'What are we going to do?' she asked. 'Baldy's sick in the head. The baby's got a fever. Betsy's worked up over her mother. We can't go on like this. We just can't.'

'I don't know,' he said angrily and, stepping around her, walked to where Clara sat beside the baby.

He had no business getting angry with Mrs. Mack, he told himself. It was just that he was frustrated. He didn't know what to do. No one else did, either. It was all wrong, he told himself. Baldy Mack should be on his feet taking the responsibility. He looked at the food piled along the wall and thought how that early in the morning none of them had dreamed it would be like this.

He guessed they had all thought the way he did. Bring in some food and water and lock themselves in here and out-wait the outlaws. But nobody had touched the food. The water was lukewarm. It was wet. That was all you could say for it. No one had mentioned being hungry and no one had taken more than a swallow or two of water.

If this went on until evening they would be drinking more water, and they would get hungry enough to eat some of the food, but he knew Mrs. Mack was right. They couldn't go on this way. It wasn't just a matter of out-waiting the outlaws. Instead, it had become a question of retaining their sanity.

The baby had dropped off to sleep, but he was restless and Johnny knew he wouldn't sleep very long, Clara looked up. She said, 'I fed him a little bit, but he wouldn't eat much. He's sick.'

'Hey. Baldy,' Chuck yelled. 'Don't go outside.'

Johnny wheeled to the door just as Baldy Mack reached it and started to lift the bar. He grabbed Mack and yanked him away from the door. 'Go on back and sit down,' he said, 'Chuck get his rifle. We can't trust him.'

Mrs. Mack was there then, taking her husband's hand. 'Come on, Baldy,' she said in a coaxing voice as if she were talking to a child.

But Baldy stood with his feet wide apart, a stubborn expression on his face. 'You can't keep me in here,' he said. 'You can't make me a prisoner. I ain't staying.'

Mack yanked his hand away from his wife's and lunged toward the door. Johnny hit him on the side of the face with an open palm, a hard, head-rattling blow that stopped him. He rubbed his cheek and looked at Johnny. He said as if he didn't believe it had happened, 'You hit me.'

'I'll hit you a hell of a lot harder if you don't go back and sit down,' Johnny said roughly. 'Now go on.'

Again Mrs, Mack took hold of his hand and this time he let her lead him back to where he had been sitting. The noise woke the baby who began to cry again. Clara picked him up and talked softly to him.

Johnny turned to the door and lifted the bar. 'Johnny,' Clara cried. 'What are you going to do?'

Ignoring her question, he pulled the door open and stepped outside. He called, 'I want to talk to Connor.'

'You ready to hand that dinero over?' a man shouted.

'No,' Johnny said. 'We've got a sick baby in here and want . . .'

Two guns cracked from the windows of the saloon. One bullet hit the stone wall above Johnny's head and screamed As it ricocheted across the street, the other ripped through the edge of the door beside his face, a flying splinter driving into his cheek. He jumped back inside, shutting and barring the door as the jeering sound of laghter came to him from the saloon.

'You're shot,' Clara screamed.

She ran to him and wiped the blood from the side of his face with the towel she had been using on the baby. 'No, I'm not shot,' he said. 'I guess I just proved what we knew all the time. We're staying here.'

Chuck stood beside Betsy, his rifle in one hand, Baldy Mack's in the other. He said, 'Them dirty bastards tried to kill you. While ago I was thinking we could run outside and duck around the corner. At least we'd be outside in the fresh air, but I guess we'd never get to the corner.'

Funny what a man thinks when he's under this kind of pressure, Johnny thought. What good would it do to get outside in the fresh air? But he didn't ask the question. He said, 'No, we'd never make it to the corner,' and then he wondered why he had tried to do something he had been telling Clara couldn't be done. All he knew was that he would have been killed if the outlaws had shot a little straighter.

CHAPTER SIXTEEN

Carl Sturtz was in a foul mood when he left Douglas, largely because of the way the sheriff, Abe Newel, had treated him. Now, as he rode back to Platte City and had plenty of time to think of what he had to do, the foul mood grew.

He thought again of how Newel had

appointed him deputy just to get Jake Warner and the other Platte City businessmen off his neck, and had never intended to back Sturtz up if there was trouble. He probably had not even intended for Sturtz to ever actually perform the duties of a law man.

Sturtz' opinion of himself slid a notch or two when he thought about his reasons for accepting the star. He had never intended to assume the duties of a law man any more than Newel had planned for him to.

The truth was he had liked the show of respect some of the people of Platte City had given him, the kind of respect that an old man who has lived a fruitful life expects from younger people. He figured to get what little glory there was without doing any of the work he should to earn it.

It was a hell of a note, he thought, when a man had done all he had and had reached his time of life and couldn't sit in the sun until it finally went down. Then his thoughts came to his wife. He compared her to Elsie Mills. Oh, she wasn't as loud and coarse and profane as Mrs. Mills, but they were a lot alike just the same, both dominating, bullying women. It seemed to Sturtz that his wife got worse with the years. He couldn't stand it. Not another day of living with her.

Sturtz, and he guessed nearly everyone else in Platte City, thought the same thing, figured Elsie Mills' husband had just up and died to get away from her because he couldn't do it as long as he was alive. Then, suddenly, it struck Sturtz that the same avenue of escape was open to him. As a matter of fact, it was not only open; it was actually waiting for him in the person of Black Jack Connor.

He began to laugh. He laughed so hard that tears rolled down his cheeks and he had to wipe his eyes with his bandanna. He hadn't laughed this hard for years, but it was the damnedest joke he had ever heard of. Everything was set up for him. He would go back to Platte City and root Black Jack out of town, or try to, and in the process he would get killed.

He could picture his wife when she heard the news. She'd say, 'He just did it to spite me. He never gave a thought to what would happen to me after he was gone. How am I going to live now?'

And another thing. It would play hell with Abe Newell's reputation. It might be enough to beat him if anybody had enough guts to run against him.

When it got around over the county that he had failed to support his deputy by refusing to quit his poker game and his deputy had gone after a gang of bank robbers lone-handed and got himself killed, well, it would show Newel up for the coward he was. And as for Carl Sturtz, why, folks would remember some of the things he had done as a younger man that had been forgotten and his name would become a legend.

Then the laughter died. Suddenly he remembered the seven people who were penned up in the stone jail. Getting himself killed might answer his personal problems, but it sure wouldn't get those folks out of jail. When he thought about spending the whole day in that stone oven of a jail, with the dust like it was and all, he decided it was enough to make them go crazy.

Not that he worried about the lives of his friends. Black Jack and his outlaw pack couldn't get at them as long as they stayed inside the jail, but there was the danger of them panicking and leaving the safety of jail without giving any thought to what would happen to them. He had known people to do that. He had promised to bring a posse, hopefully by noon, and it was after that now.

He knew then he had better do some worrying about the people in the jail. No, getting killed wasn't the answer, but he didn't know what the answer was. He did know one thing. Bulling right into it and capturing Black Jack and his gang was out of the question.

For a time he was caught in a bog of indecision, his plans continuing to reverse themselves. As a law man, he had a duty to the people in the jail, and that was where he ran head-on into a blank wall.

By this time the outlaws would be half

drunk on Limpy Smith's liquor and they would have finished Elsie Mills' dinner. What was worse, they would be impatient. They wouldn't have the money. Sturtz had a great deal of respect for Johnny Roan. He would bet his bottom dollar that Johnny would hang onto the bank's money.

The outlaws would also know that sooner or later a posse from the West would catch up with them. He had no idea what Black Jack and his men would do, but with the situation the way it was, he was certain the outlaws would do something drastic to get their hands on the bank's money.

He was almost in town when he heard two shots. He couldn't even guess what they meant, but they meant something, probably bad. They came from somewhere along Main Street, and that was the last place he wanted to be.

So, because all of his thinking had brought him exactly nowhere, he decided he would swing south of town and come in from the back sides of the bank, the store, and the jail. There were no windows or doors on the rear wall of the jail. None on the two sides, either, but he could talk to Johnny through one of the loopholes and find out what had happened. The outlaws would probably be in the saloon across the street, so the chance of them seeing him seemed slim.

He took a good deal of time to make the

swing through the sagebrush. When he finally reached a point south of town where he thought it was safe to make the move toward the jail, he realized that he was taking a risk to come in on his horse. He would be easily seen if any of the outlaws were in the back of the store or the café.

As soon as he reached the first cabin, he dismounted and left his horse in the shed behind it. He pulled his rifle from the boot, and as he moved around the cabin, he heard two more shots. For a time he stood with his back against the cabin wall so he wouldn't stand out above the sagebrush and attract anyone's attention who happened to be looking in his direction.

Carefully he scanned the rear of every building on the south side of Main Street, but he caught no movement, no pace of life. Some of Elsie Mills' washing hung on the line back of the café. Baldy Mack's freight wagon had been pulled in behind the store where he had left it the night before. He hauled most of his merchandise from Douglas himself and let his wife run the store much of the time.

Nothing was wrong with any of this. As near as he could tell, everything was exactly the way it had been left the night before. He started toward the rear of the jail, his gaze whipping back and forth, still searching for anything that might have been changed or moved, or anything that might hint at the presence of any of the outlaws on this side of Main Street.

He was uneasy, although he wasn't sure why. He kept telling himself that anything that happened would be on Main Street, not back here. There was no reason for any of Black Jack's men being around the rear of these buildings, but this constant reasurrance he gave himself did not remove his uneasiness.

He moved slowly and carefully, every sense alert. All that he had learned as a law man in his younger years came back to him. One of the things he had learned was to expect the unexpected in a situation like this.

So, even though logic told him nothing would happen behind the business buildings on the south side of Main Street, the fact was that something did happen. Two men darted out of the back of the store, raced across the loading platform that ran along the entire back of the store, and went on to the rear wall of the jail.

Sturtz dived behind the woodpile that belonged to the Mack house the instant the men appeared. They were not looking for anyone back here, so he was reasonably certain he had not been seen. Still, he took his time moving around the woodpile until he had a view of the rear of the jail.

He was close enough to the men to be reasonably sure he had never seen them before, so they must be members of Black Jack Connor's gang. He raised his rifle, intending to shoot both of them, then he lowered it as he puzzled over what they were doing.

One of the men had a pick, the other a shovel. Apparently they were digging under the stone wall, so he wondered if they were trying to tunnel under it so they could crawl into the jail and shoot it out with the men inside. No, that would be suicide, and there certainly would be no attempt on the part of this gang of outlaws to commit suicide.

He saw them back away and straighten up. They tossed the pick and shovel away, then one stooped and appeared to push something under the wall. That done, they started back toward the store. Suddenly he thought he knew what they were planning, the notion sending a chill down his spine.

They intended to blow out the rear wall of the jail! Sturtz raised his rifle to shoot the outlaws, but he was slow. Both men were across the loading platform and into the store before Sturtz could squeeze off a shot.

He lowered the rifle and wiped his sweaty face with his bandanna. He could have shot both men. He guessed he had been so shocked by the monstrous thing they were planning that he had not moved as fast as he would normally have done. Maybe it was just as well. They didn't know he was here. Now that he realized what they were planning, he'd get them when they returned to fire the dynamite. What was more, he'd take pleasure in doing it.

One question nagged him and he could find no answer to it. Why hadn't they gone ahead and touched off the dynamite? Maybe Black Jack was running a bluff, hoping to scare Johnny Roan and the others out of the jail. When he remembered that Johnny had his wife and baby in there with him, he realized a bluff might work. Now that it was too late, he wished he had shot the two men when he'd had a chance.

CHAPTER SEVENTEEN

Black Jack Connor came to with a whacking headache. When he tried to sit up, he thought his skull was going to explode. He pulled himself to the wall and put his shoulders against it, then he saw Elsie Mill's body.

From a great distance he heard Cutter Doon say, 'She damned near brained you. If you didn't have a thick skull and if you hadn't had your hat on, I figure she would have.'

Black lack felt gingerly of his head, then gripped a corner of the work table and pulled himself to his feet. He was remembering now, the bank money that was in the jail and the stubborn people who had refused to turn it over; he remembered Billy Horn and his rebellion which would come to the surface any time. He also remembered that he had sent

Miggs into the store to find some dynamite.

He asked, 'What happened?'

'She yanked a frying pan off the stove and knocked you in the head,' Doon answered. 'Then I shot her.'

First Limpy Smith and then this woman! He leaned against the wall, shutting his eyes until the wave of nausea passed. It wouldn't take much to bring his dinner up. He asked, 'How long was I on the floor?'

'I dunno,' Cutter Doon answered. 'Maybe ten minutes.'

'We can't waste any more time,' Black Jack said. 'Get over to the store. If Miggs has found the dynamite, go to the back of the jail and plant it under the rear wall, then go back to the store. I'll give 'em one more chance. If they don't hand the money over, we'll blow out the rear wall. I'll send a couple of boys to the store and you four can go into the jail from the back. I don't look for no trouble once we blow that back wall out. The whole shebang may fall down, so it could turn out to be a proposition of moving a lot of rock to find the dinero.'

Cutter Doon chewed on his lower lip a moment, then he said, 'I don't think you'll be able to get back to the saloon. You look purty wobbly to me.'

'I'll make it,' Black Jack said. 'Get a move on.'

He reeled out of the kitchen, grabbed the counter in the dining room until the world quit whirling in front of him, then went on to the street door. Again he had to stop until the dizziness passed. When it was gone, he left the café and walked to the corner, keeping close to the walls of buildings so he couldn't be seen from the jail.

So far the people in the jail had not fired a shot, but sooner or later they would when they decided time had run out on them. He was surprised they hadn't started shooting before this. In any case, there was no sense in taking chances. For a moment he rested at the corner until he felt he could cross the street on the run. There would be that moment before he reached the opposite corner when he would be visible to anyone in the jail who was watching, one short moment when he could be shot to death. If he were one of the men in the jail, that was exactly the moment he would be waiting for, but the people in the jail were not killers, and that was their weakness.

He crossed the street on the run and leaned against the east wall of the corner building as soon as he was out of sight from the jail. He remained there several minutes until he had his strength back, then he went on along the east side of the building and down the alley to the saloon.

When he went in, he saw that all of the men had been drinking. Billy Horn faced him, one hand on the butt of his gun. He was more belligerent than ever. He started to say something, but Black Jack beat him to it. He said, 'Cutter and Miggs are planting the dynamite under the back wall of the jail. It's just a matter of minutes now.'

He hoped he was right. He didn't know what would happen if he wasn't, but it wouldn't be to his liking. He had been able to put off his reckoning with Billy Horn and he hoped he could continue to do so until this building was settled, but now, looking at Horn, he wasn't sure. Horn stood motionless, his hand still on the butt of his gun. A combination of whisky and temper might trigger Horn into action.

Black Jack turned to the bar and had a quick drink. It helped his headache and wiped out the last of the dizziness. He went to the door and called, 'Cutter, have you got that dynamite set?'

Doon showed himself in the store doorway. He called back, 'It's ready. You want us to blow it?'

'We'll give these fools one more chance,' Black Jack said. 'You people in the jail, you listen and listen good. We're done fooling with you. We'll wait five minutes for you to come out with the dinero. If you don't, we'll blow up the back wall of the jail and the chances are the whole building will go down on top of you.'

He turned back to face the men who had gathered behind Billy Horn. He said, 'I told Cutter I'd send two men to the store to go with him and Miggs into the jail from the back as soon as the dynamite goes off. Slim and Big Nose, you're the stoutest men in the bunch. This may call for some stout men if you have to lift part of the wall off the money. I look for it to be one hell of a mess once that rear wall is gone.' He motioned to the store across the street. 'Go on.'

Black Jack walked to the bar and poured another drink. He felt relieved, as if he had been reaching for something that had been just beyond his finger tips, but now had it. Everything was going to be all right. His thinking earlier in the day about this being the end of the road for him was crazy. He'd get out of town with the rest of his . . .

He had lifted the glass of whisky almost to his mouth when he heard a burst of rifle fire from the jail. He threw the glass down and wheeled to the door. Slim and Big Nose lay in the dust of the street. They were dead. He didn't need to go out and feel their pulse. He had seen too many dead men to be mistaken about them.

The damned fools! He thought all of the men knew how to cross to the store. He hadn't thought it was necessary to give instructions, but Slim and Big Nose had tried to go directly from the saloon to the store. The men in the jail had finally decided it was time to shoot.

He felt his pulse pounding at his temples; he felt Billy Horn's eyes boring into his back, and he could imagine Horn saying that if he hadn't piddled around all day, Slim and Big Nose would be alive and they'd have the money and they'd all be on their way out of town.

'Fire it, Cutter,' Black Jack yelled. 'Blow 'em to hell. You hear me?'

'I hear you,' Cutter yelled back.

'Now you bastards in the jail come out of there,' Black Jack bellowed. 'Come out with your hands up. The first one who comes through the door had better be holding the dinero in front of him. You've got about sixty seconds before that dynamite goes off.'

He stood watching the front of the jail, but the door didn't open.

CHAPTER EIGHTEEN

Johnny Roan, standing beside one of the windows of the jail, could see the bodies of the two outlaws lying in the street in front of the saloon. He had shot one and Chuck Morgan the other. Now, thinking back over what had happened since Chuck had brought word about his grandfather's death early that morning, Johnny wished he'd started shooting when Black Jack Connor had led his men past the jail. They could have shot three or more of the gang before they found cover. It might have been enough to send the rest of them on their way immediately.

That was what Chuck had wanted to do, but no, Johnny had to play it close to his chest the way Carl Sturtz had said. He knew now it had been wrong. If they had made it too hot for the remaining outlaws to stay in town, they could have saved themselves these long, hot hours in the jail and the baby's fever and maybe Baldy Mack's breakdown or whatever it was. Perhaps Limpy Smith and Elsie Mills would be alive.

But there was no sense in thinking about what might have been. Johnny had his rifle on the ready, his eyes fixed on the front of the saloon. He'd shoot anybody who showed his nose. Hindsight had taught him that much. Then he heard Connor yell to someone in the store about the dynamite. They had heard digging at the back of the jail a few minutes before and had wondered about it. Now he knew what it had meant.

He called to Mrs. Mack, 'How much dynamite did you have in the store?'

'Enough to blow us all to kingdom come,' she answered.

Johnny looked at Chuck. He asked, 'What do you make of it?'

'Looks like we're gonna get it,' the boy said hoarsely.

No one said anything for a time. Baldy Mack looked as if he had dropped off to sleep. He sat motionless, his back against the wall, his chin on his chest. Betsy and Clara were frightened and showed it. Up until this moment they had felt they were safe as long as they stayed inside, but now even that sense of security was gone. They were frozen by fear, their eyes pinned on Johnny as if expecting him to perform some kind of miracle to save them.

Finally Clara asked in a whisper, 'What will happen if they blow the jail up?'

'Maybe just the back wall will go out,' Johnny said, 'but it's sure to make a big enough hole for them to come through. Or maybe the whole building will collapse and we'll be squashed like a bunch of bugs you step on.'

He heard Connor's warning, but no one, not even Mrs. Mack, urged Johnny to heed the warning. They'd be shot as soon as they appeared in the street. She was as much convinced of that now as Johnny was.

Suddenly Mrs. Mack began to swear as convincingly as any mule-skinner Johnny had ever heard. She grabbed her husband's rifle from where Chuck leaned it against the wall and, ramming the barrel through a loophole, began to fire at the front of the saloon.

Johnny said, 'Let's help her use up a little of this ammunition, Chuck.'

He began firing at the front of the saloon. Puzzled, Chuck stared at him for a moment, then he, too, poked his rifle through a window and started to shoot. None of them could see any of the outlaws and Johnny suspected it was a waste of lead.

They were firing at an angle and all that Black Jack and his men had to do was to pull back into the saloon and be out of range. The bullets smashed the glass out of the saloon's windows and riddled the batwings, but that, Johnny thought, was about all the damage they were doing.

Mrs. Mack emptied her Winchester first and began to reload immediately, her face twisted and made ugly by the murderous fury that possessed her. Johnny stepped back from the window and reloaded, wondering why the outlaws hadn't fired the dynamite. It had been a very long sixty seconds.

He had a terrible feeling that all seven of them in the jail were waiting to die, that the roof at least would collapse on them and they'd be crushed, Clara and the baby along with the rest. But there was no alternative. Then, suddenly, the thought flashed through his mind that there was one, at least for Clara and Betsy and the baby. Mrs. Mack, too, if she wanted to go.

Chuck had started to reload and Mrs. Mack had turned to the loophole when Johnny cried out, 'Hold it. I'm going to open the door. Clara, take the baby. Betsy, go with her. As soon as we start to shoot, you run like hell around the corner to the west side of the jail and then get away from it as fast as you can.

Go anywhere except into the street. As long as we're shooting, we'll drive them back from the front of the saloon so they can't fire at you.'

'Sure,' Chuck said. 'It'll work. Why didn't we think of it before?'

'Mrs. Mack,' Johnny said, 'you go with Clara and Betsy, or stay and shoot if you want to.'

'I'm staying,' she said savagely.

Johnny lifted the bar, then stopped and stood motionless when a man yelled from the store, 'Connor, Cutter Doon's dead. We tried to get to the dynamite, but some son of a bitch back of the store started shooting at us. He got Cutter with the first shot. I made it to the store, but I'm bleeding from a bullet crease on my right shoulder.'

For a moment there was a stunned silence. Johnny said, 'So that's why the dynamite didn't go off.'

'I guess we didn't hear no shots back of the jail because of the shooting we were doing,' Chuck said.

Now Black Jack Connor recovered from the shock that the news must have given him. He bellowed, 'Go on back and fire it. It only takes one match.'

'The hell I will,' the outlaw shouted. 'That jasper shoots too straight for me. I couldn't see him. He was hidden in a cabin or shed or something, but I seen Doon go down with a slug in his head. I ain't giving that booger another whack at me.'

Silence again. Johnny picked up the bar and dropped it back into place. He looked at Chuck, then slowly brought his gaze to Clara. He said, 'I feel like a man condemned to death and then gets a reprieve with ten seconds to go. I expected that dynamite to go off before I could get you and Betsy and the baby out of here.'

Clara was sitting on her heels rocking the baby back and forth. She was crying softly, but she was able to say, 'I know, Johnny, I felt the same way.' She swallowed and wiped her eyes. The baby had worn himself out until he had dropped off into a light sleep, whimpering now and then, but not really waking up. Clara said, 'He's so hot and feverish, Johnny. If we could have got out a minute ago, why can't we go now?'

'It's too great a risk,' he said. 'Even when we're shooting at the front of the saloon, I don't know for sure we've got all of them driven back so they can't shoot at us. While ago it seemed like it was worth taking the risk.'

'How long?' Clara whispered. 'How much longer?'

'Maybe till dark,' Johnny said.

Betsy wasn't able to say anything, She stood a few feet from Chuck, her eyes shut, her lips squeezed tightly together. Mrs. Mack looked down at her husband, the rifle clutched in both hands, her face white. Suddenly she threw the Winchester to the floor and put her shoulders against the wall as she raised her hands to her face and begin to cry, making a strange, moaning sound. Johnny thought she would be the last one to break down, but the long, hot hours of waiting and worrying had finally caught up with her.

'Who do you figure was doing the shooting back of the jail?' Chuck asked.

'Must have been Sturtz,' Johnny said. 'He probably couldn't get a posse, so he came back himself.'

'I'll take a look,' Chuck said.

Johnny nodded. He stood beside the window staring at the front of the saloon. He still could not see anyone; he couldn't hear anything, but he had a tingling feeling along his backbone. Maybe the outlaws had had enough. Maybe they'd get out of town now.

The baby was awake and screaming. Clara, who had regained her composure, was not able to comfort him. Mrs. Mack walked back and forth in front of Baldy struggling for self control. Betsy still hadn't moved. Johnny, glancing at her, thought that she was paralyzed by fear.

Johnny watched the saloon. The man in the store was making no attempt to cross the street to the others in the saloon, and no one in the saloon was trying to get to the café or store. Johnny was sure he would have glimpsed them darting across the street at the end of the block if they had.

Chuck came back from the rear of the jail. 'I looked through all the loopholes, and I can't see anybody, but it don't prove anything. If it was Sturtz, he probably holed up somewhere.'

He looked at Johnny, a frightened boy who had held up his end so far, but Johnny wasn't sure how much longer he could hold up. Or any of the others if it kept on being a standoff as it had been most of the day.

He had heard of situations like this in which people had been under siege for days but had survived and maintained their sanity, and he wondered how they had done it. Was it the crying, sick baby who made the difference? Or Baldy Mack's breakdown? Or the knowledge that the men in the saloon were completely calloused and brutal?

Chuck had been looking at him. Now he asked, 'What do we do?'

'We wait,' Johnny said. 'I can think of a lot of crazy things we could try, but we're not trying any of them.'

Chuck turned to Betsy and put an arm around her as he said something to her in a low tone. Johnny wasn't sure she heard. He remained by the window, still watching the front of the saloon. It was easy to tell Chuck they would wait. The baby had been quiet for a little while. Now he began crying again. Johnny wiped his sweaty face and wondered how much longer they could wait.

CHAPTER NINETEEN

Cutter Doon was dead! Black Jack poured himself a drink and then stood staring at the amber liquid, unable to believe it was true. Doon was the only friend he had in the gang, the only man he could count on when the blue chip was down.

Sure, he had been sorry when Slim and Big Nose had been shot, not because he had any particular liking for them, but because their deaths weakened the gang. It was different with Doon. The man had come to him as soon as he'd been released from the Yuma pen. When Black Jack had said he wanted an outfit of hardcases, Doon had said he knew where to get them.

He lifted the glass and gulped the drink and set the glass back on the bar. He had always been a man to face the reality of truth and he accepted Doon's death as truth. Miggs had no reason to lie about it, but who had killed Doon and wounded Miggs? And what was he, Black Jack, going to do now?

If he crossed the street to the store, he'd be shot down the same as Slim and Big Nose had been. If he went to the end of the block and crossed over, he'd be shot by the same man who had killed Doon if he showed himself long enough to fire the dynamite.

It was a stalemate. He could hold the people in the jail, but they could stay inside and keep the money because now he had no way to force them out. Well, by God, he'd burn a little gun powder and the people in the jail would know they were stuck there and would have to go on sweating in that overheated furnace.

He drew his gun as he turned from the bar and stopped, flat-footed. Billy Horn and the rest of the men stood in front of him, all with their guns in their hands except Horn. Black Jack had forgotten about his smoldering feud with Horn. He knew now as his gaze swept their sullen, resentful faces that this was the end. His bunch was breaking up and he was helpless to prevent it.

'We're riding out,' Billy Horn said. 'We don't give a good, thin damn what you do. We don't want you with us and we don't want to be with you, and we sure as hell ain't taking no more orders from you.'

He should have expected this. Doon had helped him keep the men in line. Doon had known, too, that if the gang stayed together, Black Jack would have to take Horn down a notch. He'd do it now, but he couldn't take all of them, so he'd have to let them go. There was nothing else he could do.

'Then get out of town,' Black Jack said. 'Go on and leave that dinero in the jail. Ride out empty-handed. I don't care what you do, neither.'

Billy Horn grinned. 'Oh, that won't work, Connor. We'd like to have the money, all right, but we're glad to go empty-handed. At least we're alive, which is more than you can say for Cutter. Or Slim or Big Nose. They say you were a great outlaw in your day, but your day was a long time ago. You sure never showed anything great to us.'

Black Jack jerked his head at the back door. 'Get your horses and ride out,' he said wearily. 'I done the best I could with what I had to work with. If these boys follow you, they won't live long.'

'Come on, Billy,' one of the men said. 'This ain't getting us nowhere. All I want is to get out of this stinking town before a posse shows us.'

For a moment Billy Horn didn't move and didn't say anything. He stared at Black Jack, the corners of his mouth working, his right hand splayed above the butt of his gun. He wanted to kill Black Jack. It was in his face, it was in his eyes, it was in the way he stood there, reluctant to walk out and leave Black Jack alive and standing on his feet.

Black Jack had known moments the last day or so when he had wanted to kill Billy and had even come close to drawing on him. Now he had no interest in shooting it out with him, not when the people were still inside the jail with the money and when the man who had killed

Cutter Doon was alive. They were his enemies, not Billy Horn. He had never walked out on a job in his life and he had no intention of doing it now.

'Go on, Billy,' he said. 'Don't push me. No sense of us trying to kill each other. The men we should be killing are on the other side of the street, but before you go, I'll tell you one thing. As long as you're live, you'll never forget that you walked out and left them there in the jail, alive and kicking.'

'All right, we're going,' Horn said. 'You're an old man, Connor. The stink of death is on you. You won't live long enough to read about the banks we hold up.'

They moved to the alley door, walking backwards as they held their guns on him. He looked at them, men who had taken his orders until now, dirty, tired men with stubble-covered faces, men who had ridden with him all the way from Arizona to Platte City, Wyoming. It was the first time in his career as an outlaw leader that he had ever had his men desert him.

It hurt, but he lifted a hand in a farewell gesture as he said, 'So long, boys.'

None of them said a word or made a gesture of any kind. They went out through the door and into the alley. A moment later he heard their pounding steps as they ran toward the livery stable for their horses.

He moved to the front of the saloon and

looked through a window, the glass smashed out of it by the flurry of gunfire that had broken out a few minutes before. He stared across the street at the front of the jail, knowing there was no way he could get to Miggs or Miggs could get to him without great risk. Probably it didn't make any difference. If Miggs had been there, he would have left with Billy Horn and the other.

For a moment his eyes were fixed on the dead men in the street, then he turned his gaze to the stone front of the jail again. He cursed the dead men for getting themselves killed, he cursed himself, he cursed the men in the jail, and finally he cursed the man who had shot Cutter Doon.

He heard Billy Horn and the rest of them ride past the rear of the saloon. They would head for the mountains. In a few hours, if their tired horses held up, they would be having that cold drink of water he had been wanting.

Once more the knowledge came to him that this was the end of the track for him, Black Jack Connor. Billy Horn had been right. The stink of death was on him. He would never leave this hot, dusty little Wyoming town alive.

His mind had gone full circle. He had known earlier in the day that this was the final focus, and then later he had been dead sure he would get the money after he had thought about blowing out the back of the jail. After that he had expected to be riding out of town

145

about this time at the head of his gang with Cutter Doon beside him.

Sure, he could get his horse and take the same trail Billy Horn and the others were riding, but what was the use? There was nothing left for him, nothing but to wait until they tried to root him out, and then he would make them sorry they had killed Cutter Doon.

He couldn't run any more. It was better to make his stand here than to try to get out of the country on a horse that didn't have more than a few miles left in him. Billy Horn and the others would find that out in a few days. They'd die with a rope around their necks, but not Black Jack Connor.

So he waited by the window for the people to come out of the jail. They would have to sooner or later, and when they did, he would kill them all.

CHAPTER TWENTY

Chuck Morgan was the one who saw the outlaws run along the alley from the rear of the saloon to the livery stable. He had been standing by a window, holding Betsy's hand and looking across the street when several men raced past the vacant lot between the stable and the saloon.

For a moment the boy was too surprised to

do anything. They appeared suddenly and then they were gone. He blinked and wondered if he had imagined it, then knew he hadn't. He dropped Betsy's hand and wheeled away from the window.

'Johnny,' Chuck called, 'I just seen a bunch of them hardcases head for the stable. A whole passel of 'em, five or six.'

It took Johnny a moment to digest this fact, then he blurted, 'They must be riding out. They've had enough.'

'Then we can get out of here,' Chuck said.

Johnny joined him at the window. 'Not just yet. Now exactly how many were there, five or six?'

'I dunno,' Chuck said. 'They went by in a bunch. I couldn't count 'em. I didn't anyhow.'

Johnny counted on his fingers. Two dead men in the street. One dead man back of the store. One man marooned in the store. There had been ten in the bunch to start with. That left six of them on the north side of Main Street. If six left the saloon for the horses, that would be all of them.

Johnny didn't think the outlaws would ride out and leave the man in the store. But maybe they would. Outlaws can panic as well as anyone, and the attempted bank robbery had gone about as bad as it could for them.

The door of the livery stable was open, but no one in the jail could see all the way to the back. Johnny thought he caught movement at the far end of the runway. He guessed he had imagined it. From where he stood at one of the jail windows, he could see only the front of the runway and the first three or four stalls.

A few minutes later the outlaws rode past the vacant lot on the dead run. They were bunched, and although Johnny was looking right at them, he realized as soon as they had disappeared that he couldn't be sure whether he had seen five or six of them.

Clara came to stand beside Johnny. She held the baby, his head on her right shoulder. She was dead tired. So was the baby. He wasn't asleep and he wasn't crying, but he was making a soft, moaning sound.

'He's all in,' Clara said wearily. 'He's too hot and sick to go to sleep, and he's cried so much today he doesn't have the strength to cry any more.'

'It won't be much longer,' Johnny said. 'I don't know whether any of them are still in the saloon or not, but I'm going to find out. If I go out and I don't get shot, you'll know they're all gone.'

Clara gripped his arm. 'No, Johnny. We've waited this long. We can wait a little longer.'

Mrs. Mack left Baldy and came to Johnny. She said, 'This has been one hell of a day. I didn't have the slightest notion when it started this morning that it would be like this, but after living through those few minutes when we thought they were blowing the jail up, I figure we can live through anything and that includes a little more waiting. Johnny, don't go out there.'

Betsy and Chuck nodded. Clara said, 'It'll he dark pretty soon. We can all get out of here then.'

'No,' Johnny said. 'All day I've leaned over backwards being careful. I know how though it's been on all of us, frying like we have in here. It's time we're getting out. There can't be more than one man left in the saloon. The one in the store can't do anything unless I show myself in front of him.'

He lifted the bar, set it down, and pulled the door open. He stepped out into the patch of shadow in front of the jail. A gun roared from the saloon immediately and Johnny wheeled and lunged back inside. The bullet had ripped into the casing about a foot from his head.

'Well,' Johnny said, grinning at Clara as he rubbed the side of his head. 'I guess we know now. There's still one man in the saloon.'

'After all that's happened and we know we're safe,' Clara said, 'you don't have to be a hero.'

'A hero is one thing I'll never be,' Johnny said. 'Next time I'm going out of here on the run and get around the corner of the jail to the side. If it was Sturtz who downed the man that tried to fire the dynamite, I'll find him and . . .'

'Johnny.'

Johnny stopped talking and cocked his

head, wondering who had called his name. He realized that it had not been anyone inside the jail. Someone must be trying to get his attention from one of the loopholes. He started toward the west wall, still puzzled, not sure that whoever had called was on the side of the building.

'Here,' the voice said. 'The loophole nearest the front of the building. It's me, Carl Sturtz.'

'Well, we're glad to see you,' Johnny said.

Actually he couldn't see much through the small hole, but it was Sturtz's voice, so there could be no doubt of the man's identity. Sturtz asked, 'How has it been going for you?'

'It's hot as hell in here,' Johnny answered. 'I guess they've murdered Limpy Smith and Elsie Mills. We don't know for sure, but we heard some shots while ago.' He hesitated, then asked, 'Did you see them ride out?'

'Yeah, I seen 'em,' the old man said, 'and then I heard the shot, so I figure one of 'em is still over there. I'm guessing it's Connor unless one of 'em is wounded and can't ride. Connor was always a stubborn cuss, so he just wouldn't leave with the others. At least that's the way it looks to me.'

'Where's the posse you were bringing to town?' Johnny asked.

Sturtz cursed, then he said, 'Abe Newel was playing poker in Douglas. He was a little drunk and he said I was lying and there wasn't no danger here. He wouldn't do anything, so I

150

came back to see what I could do.'

For an old man who had been called a has-been, this took a lot of guts, Johnny thought. He said, 'I guess you were the one who kept us from being blowed to kingdom come while ago.'

'It was me, all right,' Sturtz said. 'I circled town and came in from the south. I seen them two digging under your back wall, but it took me a while to figure out what they were up to. I let both of 'em get into the store, but when they came back, I got one of 'em good and clipped the other one. I should of nailed him, but damn it, he moved purty fast.'

'I'd call it good shooting to get one of 'em,' Johnny said, 'but we're still penned up here. I figured I'd try to get out again, but as long as that bastard is sitting there waiting for me, it's a little risky. I think I can make it, though. A couple of rifles blasting at the front of the jail will drive him back . . .'

'Maybe,' Sturtz said, 'and maybe not. As long as Black Jack Connor is alive, he's as dangerous as any sidewinder you ever seen. You never know for sure what he's going to do.' He paused, then added, 'I guess it's up to me to root him out.'

'You'd have to cross the street,' Johnny said.

'Yep,' Sturtz said. 'It's the only way to get at him. It had better be me instead of you. I don't much care whether I live or don't live, but I'd kind of like to get Connor so I can jam his carcass down Newel's throat.'

Johnny shook his head. 'Unless we can keep him in the back of the saloon, he'll pick you off before you get across the street. You'd better try the other end of the block. That's the way they've been doing it except for them two that's lying in the street. You'll be at enough of an angle that you'll probably get across before he catches a glimpse of you.'

'No, I figure my best chance is right here,' Sturtz said. 'The sooner I do it the better. I'll lose my courage if I think about it long enough. You and Chuck start shooting. You'll keep him back so he won't see me.'

'If he stays there,' Johnny said,

'That's the chance I'll have to take,' Sturtz said. 'Now get at it.'

Johnny turned from the loophole. He said, 'Let's start burning some powder again. Sturtz is going after him.'

'He's more man than I ever gave him credit for,' Mrs Mack said.

She picked up Baldy's rifle and moved to the loophole where she had stood before when she had shot at the saloon. She waited until Johnny and Chuck were ready. Johnny said, 'Let him have it,' and pulled the trigger.

The crash of the rifles was deafening, all three firing rapidly until their Winchesters were empty. Johnny caught a glimpse of Sturtz, bending low and running hard across the street and through the livery stable door.

Now it was up to the old man. If he failed, it would be Johnny's turn. One thing was certain. Black Jack Connor had to die within the next few minutes. If he didn't, Carl Sturtz and Johnny Roan would.

CHAPTER TWENTY-ONE

Carl Sturtz plunged through the archway of the livery stable and turned to lean against the wall of a stall, breathing hard, the cracking of rifles from the jail pounding against his ears. He had not forced his ancient legs into a run for years, and now he felt the muscles of his legs jerking. He wasn't sure they were going to hold him. Blood was pounding in his arteries, too, and for a time the stable floor tipped and turned and whirled in front of him.

He didn't have time to stay here until he was rested. Johnny Roan had been right. Connor might not remain in the saloon, but the real reason to hurry was that Sturtz had to get it over with. He had built himself up for this and he could not risk a let down.

It would not be a gun duel when he tackled Connor, but a simple proposition of shooting first and shooting straighter. That was the code by which Black Jack Connor lived, and so it had to be Sturtz's code, too.

He started along the runway toward the

alley, his gun in his right hand. He was still breathing hard, but his heart had slowed down and his leg muscles had stopped twitching. For an instant he thought of his wife and what she would say if she knew what he was doing, but he dismissed the thought at once. From now on, if he lived, everything was going to be different.

His gaze swept the alley. It was empty. He hurried toward the rear of the saloon, moving past the empty lot between it and the stable. When he reached the loading platform of the saloon, he saw Limpy Smith's body where the outlaws had left it in the dirt and weeds at the base of the platform.

Sturtz stepped up to the loading platform, knowing he would not soon forget the gruesome sight of Smith's eyes staring unseeingly at the sky. He threaded his way through the beer barrels to the back door of the saloon. Limpy Smith had not been a great man by any stretch of the imagination, but he did not deserve to be murdered and thrown into an alley and left there for flies to crawl over his face.

Sturtz cocked his gun, having no doubt that Elsie Mills had suffered the same fate Smith had, or possibly a worse one. He eased into the saloon, his gaze sweeping the big room. The rifles in the jail had been silent for some time. For a moment Sturtz did not see anyone. He felt his pulse pounding again and he had the terrible thought that if anyone else was in the saloon, the hammering of his heart would give his presence away.

Then he spotted Connor hunched down at the side of one of the street windows, his gun in his hand. The man was looking for something, or maybe just staring at the front of the jail, but apparently he had not heard Sturtz come in.

For a little while Sturtz had a faint hope he could take the man alive. He called, 'Hook the moon, Connor. Drop your gun. You make any kind of a move and I'll kill you.'

His voice sounded very loud in his ears. A little quavery, too, as if he were scared. He was, scared that Connor would whirl and fire. It would be too much to expect for the outlaw just to give up. He certainly knew that if he were captured, he would hang.

The seconds dragged by. Connor didn't move. He didn't even act as if he had heard. Sturtz wondered if the man were deaf, or maybe he had been shot and had died and somehow had leaned against the wall in that position. No, that was ridiculous. Then Sturtz had the notion that maybe he hadn't said anything. He just thought he had.

He started toward Connor, puzzled and a little confused, then Connor did exactly what Sturtz had been afraid he would. He came around very fast like a tightly coiled spring that has suddenly been released. He fired; Sturtz saw the red tongue of powerflame leap from the muzzle of the outlaw's revolver and the great cloud of smoke and he heard the roar of the shot. The bullet didn't miss him by more than an inch or two, then his own gun was bucking in his hand.

Connor was knocked back against the wall by Sturtz's first shot. For an instant he hung there, his gun going off again, but the strength he needed to hold it level was gone from him. The bullet plowed into the floor ten feet in front of him.

Sturtz pulled the trigger again, and then a third time. Connor's feet slid out from under him and he sat down hard, his back still against the wall, then he went over sideways, his gun spilling from his fingers.

Slowly Sturtz paced toward him, his gun still covering the outlaw. When he reached him, he kicked the dropped revolver across the room, then bent over Connor's body and reached for his wrist, but there was not even the hint of a pulse. One bullet had caught him in the stomach, another a little higher in his chest, and the third apparently had been a clean miss.

Black Jack Connor was dead. Now, staring down at the muscular body with its huge head and thick neck, Sturtz could not find any resemblance to the tough kid he had arrested a long time ago.

Then Carl Sturtz, who had not shot at a

man for a long time and had not killed one for an even longer time, realized that he, an old, worn out lawman who was wearing a deputy's star because no one else wanted it, had just shot and killed a notorious outlaw and had brought this day's trouble to an end.

He straightened his shoulders and ejected the empty shells and thumbed new loads into the cylinder. He thought with pride: *By God, I'm not worn out and Abe Newel is going to know it.* He stepped to the door and called, 'Johnny, it's all clear here, but we've still got one man in the store to root out.'

'I won't give you no trouble,' the man in the store said as he tossed his gun belt into the street. 'I'm coming out.'

He did, his hands in the air. Sturtz stepped out of the saloon as the jail door opened and Johnny Roan came through it. He asked, 'All the dust settled?'

'All settled,' Sturtz said. 'I'll lock this piece of carrion up. We'll take him to the county jail later on.'

Johnny was holding the sack of money. His wife came behind him carrying the baby who was whimpering a little, then Betsy Mills and Chuck Morgan stepped into the street. Sturtz, looking at them, had a strange feeling they were moving from prison to freedom, even from death to life.

For a moment all four simply stood motionless, looking around and breathing deeply of the hot afternoon air, their long shadows falling in front of them on the white dust of the street. A moment later the Macks left the jail, Baldy walking slowly and jerkily the way a man does who has had a stroke. He looked at Sturtz, his eyes glassy and expressionless. His wife, holding an arm and talking softly to him, led him past the others, then turned along the side of the jail and moved on toward their house.

'What's the matter with Baldy?' Sturtz asked. 'I never seen him look like that before.'

'He's sick,' Johnny said. 'Chuck, bring the guns out of the jail and stack them in front. There's plenty of water and grub inside. Let's lock this man up and let him sweat like we've been doing.'

'Betsy, you're coming home with me,' Clara said. 'Don't go into the café. Johnny will see how it is.'

The girl nodded and the two women walked quickly down the street. Johnny went on to the bank as Chuck carried the guns outside and went back for the shells. When he came out the second time, Sturtz motioned for the outlaw to go in. As soon as he was inside, Sturtz shut the door and snapped the padlock.

'That'll hold him,' Sturtz said with satisfaction. 'Well, I guess we've got some bodies to move. Maybe we'd better just lay 'em on the saloon floor till . . .'

'Company's coming,' Chuck broke in,

motioning east along Main Street toward Douglas.

Sturtz looked up to see Abe Newel leading a band of armed men into town. Some distance behind them were Jake Warner and Sturtz's wife in a buggy.

Sturtz whistled and said sourly, 'Help coming, now that we don't need it.'

He stepped into the middle of the street and walked toward the approaching posse, moving past the bodies of the two outlaws that still lay where they had fallen. When he was ten feet from the sheriff, he held up a hand for the posse to stop. He looked at Newel and shook his head in disgust.

'You sure are a hell of a sheriff, Newel,' Sturtz said.

Newel was looking past him at the dead men, then his gaze slowly came to Sturtz. He took his bandanna out of his pocket and wiped his red face. He said uneasily, 'I guess I should have come when you asked me to. Mrs. Sturtz and Jake Warner kept nagging me until we did.'

'We don't need you,' Sturtz said hotly. 'Four of Connor's gang are dead including Connor and one's locked up in jail. The reward belongs to us and don't you forget it. Black Jack ought to worth a purty good figure.'

'I ain't augerin' about the reward,' Newel said.

'Five of 'em got away,' Sturtz went on. 'You

might just as well go back to your poker game because you'll never catch the ones that pulled out, moving the way you do. Before you go, I want you to know that I'm running against you in the next election and I'll see that everybody in the county knows how you backed up your deputy today. I'm still a purty damned good man and I'll sure make a better sheriff than you are.'

Newel's face turned a darker red until it was close to purple. He started to say something, but the words wouldn't come. He swung his horse around and started back to Douglas, his men following. The last two were snickering, and as they turned, one of them said to Sturtz, 'I've got a hunch you'll beat him.'

Johnny came out of the café, his face grave. 'They shot Elsie Mills, all right. We knew they had, but I guess we just kept hoping. You'd better go tell Betsy, Chuck.'

The boy nodded and started down the street. The buggy came on, Jake Warner shouting. 'Where's the money, Johnny? Where's the money?'

This was exactly like Jake Warner, Sturtz thought. He felt like dragging the banker out of the buggy and shaking him until his teeth rattled. He said, 'Jake, you are the most cold-blooded, money-grubbing bastard I ever seen in my life. Did it ever occur to you that Johnny might have been killed? His wife and baby, too? Or that you might give him a reward for saving your bank for you?'

Warner's mouth sagged open. Sturtz guessed he had never been talked to that way before in his life. Mrs. Sturtz was equally dumbfounded. She cried, 'Carl, have you gone out of your mind, talking to Mr. Warner that way?'

'Oh, shut up,' he said wearily. 'I've got something to tell you, too. From now on I'm wearing the pants again. I dunno why I ever let you have them. I aim to run for sheriff and when I'm elected, I'll hire Johnny for my deputy. Now you can either go home and behave like a wife ought to or live by yourself. There's a cot in the stable. I can make out by myself all right.'

Mrs. Sturtz started to cry. Sturtz said, 'Get down out of that buggy and go home and finish your bawling. I'l be in after while. You'd better have supper ready when I get there.'

She stepped down from the buggy and looked at Sturtz reproachfully, but she found no comfort in his face. She walked away, holding a handkerchief to her eyes.

'The bank's money is in the safe, Mr. Warner,' Johnny said. 'You can take care of things. I'm quitting. I'll stop by in the morning and you can pay me what I've got coming.'

He walked past the buggy. Warner had been sitting there, the lines in his hands, straight-backed as if he had been frozen in the seat. He tried to speak and swallowed and finally got it out. 'Wait, Johnny. You can't quit.' Johnny turned to look at him. He added quickly, 'I'll raise your salary one dollar a week.'

Johnny laughed scornfully. He said, 'Mr. Warner, I have never been a deputy, but I can do the work, and I will unless you double my salary.'

Warner looked as if he was going to be sick. He wiped a hand across his face and took a deep breath. Then he said slowly and reluctantly, 'All right, Johnny. I'll do it.'

'I'll be at work in the morning,' Johnny said. 'Carl, I'll help you move the bodies to wherever you want them.'

'We'll put 'em in the saloon for now,' Sturtz said. As they walked back along the street, he said, 'Well Johnny, they say that sometimes all it takes to straighten things out are a few funerals.'

'Then everything must be straightened out in Platte City,' Johnny said. 'We're having the funerals.'

Sturtz glanced back at Jake Warner who hadn't moved out of his buggy. The banker had not mentioned any reward. If any man deserved it, Johnny did. He said, 'I don't want to seem hard to satisfy, but I wish we were having one more.'

We hope you have enjoyed this Large Print book. Other Chivers Press or G.K. Hall & Co. Large Print books are available at your library or directly from the publishers.

For more information about current and forthcoming titles, please call or write, without obligation, to:

Chivers Press Limited
Windsor Bridge Road
Bath BA2 3AX
England
Tel. (01225) 335336

OR

Thorndike Press
295 Kennedy Memorial Drive
Waterville
Maine 04901
USA

All our Large Print titles are designed for easy reading, and all our books are made to last.